Painted with Good Intentions

DOROTHEA ANNA

Philotimo Press

Acknowledgments

I thank God for giving me my creative writing ability, first and foremost. The support of my family and friends is a constant that is a treasure in my life. I thank my editor, D. A. Sarac, for all her amazing work. My critique partners are a great group of encouraging and awesome people: Ellie, Paul C., Trisha, and Michelle. What blessings!

To my family and friends who believe in the supernatural and love to travel.

Contents

Chapter One

Eight Months Ago

S he never should have married him. He'd been wrong, all wrong for her.

Christina walked through the empty house full of shadows and loss, her footsteps echoing on the hardwood floor, as if punctuating the ache in her heart.

She passed the kitchen, the spicy aroma of *souzoukakia* floating through her memories. The wood-topped island where she would chop the vegetables and meats was bare, across from the stainless steel appliances and abandoned breakfast nook. The grooves of the table and chairs' legs that had been there left a faint, darker tint to the faux-tiled linoleum floor.

Christina moved down the hall toward their bedroom but paused at the door on her left. She closed her eyes and swallowed hard and blindly felt for the doorframe. Biting her lip, she peeked in the small room, its blinds closed, locking out the afternoon sun. Yet slivers of light streamed through the sides of the blinds, splashing white slits on the walls. The room looked sterile, as if it'd been robbed of life. And hadn't it? Hadn't she?

She blew out a breath and strode to the bedroom, determined

to get on with what she needed to do. She grabbed her suitcase sitting on the empty room's floor, as well as her large art bag and purse, and draped them over each shoulder.

The front door creaked open. "Christina, you ready?" her best friend Becky called.

Christina walked toward the front door, her chin lifted and back straight.

Becky stood at the entryway, leaning a hand on the doorknob.

Clearing her throat, Christina nodded. "I'm ready."

They left the house and headed to their vehicles that were full of small furniture originally Christina's and a few items that used to belong to her parents.

As Becky got into her Dodge pickup truck, Christina climbed into her SUV. She glanced one last time at the olive-colored ranch home with its gaping windows and hollowed porch, invaded by weeds and uncut grass.

The past four years of Christina's life in that structure now looked bizarre to her, even as the waves of both happy and painful memories rolled through her.

Becky's truck rumbled to life, prompting Christina to start her own vehicle. She trailed her friend down the familiar street toward her new beginning.

Present Day

CHRISTINA THREW BUNDLES OF CLOTHES INTO HER SUITCASE. SHE'D managed to get three weeks off from Burton & Company for a long-awaited vacation to Greece and the island of Santorini. Her parents had graciously gifted her this needed getaway. She'd hugged them long and hard, their support of her always present throughout her life, despite whatever misjudgments she'd made. To make the holiday even sweeter, her best friend was going with her. What could be better?

The beach, sun, touring churches, and shopping lay ahead. She'd also set aside a good amount of time for sketching and watercoloring, her favorite hobbies that plucked her out of stressful situations and set her gently in her happy place. The past couple of years, she'd immersed herself in her art, locked away in that small room, a salve on her wounds.

Christina pulled underwear from her dresser drawer and froze. A bent photo was taped to the other end of the drawer. The picture of her ex-husband Justin, with his ash-blond hair, overly sensuous mouth, and deceiving brown eyes glared at her. She grimaced and pressed a hand to her queasy stomach. Justin had placed the picture there a year and a half ago, thinking it would spark longing for him. It hadn't. She rubbed her upset stomach. How had she missed it when clearing out her things for the move? She could have sworn she'd thrown every picture of him in the trash tote at the old house. Pursing her lips, Christina pulled the photograph off the wood backing, ripped it up, and threw it in the wastebasket near her desk.

Maybe the picture was a sign, a sign of her egregious decision. A decision that had come too quickly, swept up in the perceived whirl of romance and love. Meeting Justin had taken her off the path she'd planned for herself since her late teens.

On the left-hand side of her desk sat the tiny porcelain church her mother had picked up for her when she went to one of the local Greek festivals two summers ago. A perfect reminder of her earlier plans before her disastrous mistake. When she returned from this vacation, she'd search out a women's monastery and inquire about becoming a novice, if they'd accept her. Perhaps with her artistic talent, she could become an iconographer. Just about every monastery had them.

Seven peach-colored candles in round glass holders lined the top of her bureau. She lit them every evening and enjoyed their tangerine scent that would linger in her room. Christina blew out the few still flickering. She'd have to pick up some while in Greece. A room wasn't complete without candles twinkling and their delicious citrus fragrance drifting through the space. The ambiance never failed to lift her spirits.

Becky appeared at her doorway. Her long, fiery red hair was pulled back in a ponytail, and she wore jean shorts and a white T-shirt with the words SMALL BUT FULL OF SPUNK written in hot pink across her chest. She chewed on a large wad of bubble gum.

"Hey. You about ready?"

"Yeah." Christina zipped the suitcase closed, then grabbed her bulky art bag and purse.

"We should've been on the road by now."

"We're not late. We're fine."

"You know I like to be early," Becky said, popping her gum.

Christina smiled and shook her head. "I've known you forever, and you're still the most impatient person."

Becky cocked a brow. "You know this, but you still keep me waiting."

"I'll work on it."

"You've been working on it since we were goofy teens."

She waved her hands in a shooing motion toward Becky. "We're wasting time arguing, silly."

Tomorrow afternoon, Christina and her friend would be traipsing through the crowded Athens streets. Streets filled with colorful shops and ornate churches and good memories from an earlier time. She'd left a huge space in her suitcase for souvenirs and would fill it with as many artistic, religious, and historical goodies as possible.

NATHAN STUFFED THE LAST PIECE OF CLOTHING INTO HIS LUGGAGE. He was more than ready for a vacation. Time off from working with his hands, loosening people's tight muscles, to using his hands for creating art, his passion.

He unzipped the middle compartment of his suitcase.

Although he'd prefer to be in the mountains instead of near

the sea, he appreciated the stunning beauty of Santorini. He carefully placed his art supplies into his pochade, then slid it into his bag, as his mind wandered to the breathtaking views and the cozy villages among the bustling and pulsating towns clustered on the apexes of the rocky island.

Catching up with his *Thío* Ioannis by doing some murals and painting in his shop would be one of the highlights of the trip. It had been nearly five years since he'd seen his uncle. That was more recent than visiting his grandfather. But he'd meet up with Papou in Athens after his time on Santorini.

He'd been thirteen the last time he'd stayed several weeks at his grandfather's house. The childhood memories of spending quality time with his grandfather ran through his mind—when Papou had taken him to the local park where he'd jump on the merry-go-round, crawl across a jungle gym, and throw pebbles into the ocean waves. Nathan could still smell the pungent, salty air.

He zipped the bag closed. He would find a time midway through his relaxing on Santorini to create the special painting for his grandfather.

"It's showtime, Nate." His best friend, George, filled the doorframe to his bedroom. "We're free, man. And there are loads of gorgeous Mediterranean beauties in Greece."

Nathan followed George to his Toyota pickup truck. He didn't have the same ideas about this trip, but when had he and George ever lined up on interests? Women were all George thought about. Granted, his friend had a point. There were gorgeous women in Greece, but searching for women on the island wasn't in his plans. His last romantic relationship had left him with little interest in going down that path again anytime soon. Painting would fill most of his days. It always gave him a venue to release his stress and delve into a calming space.

George jabbed an elbow into Nathan's ribs. "I know you're still bummed over Jennifer, but think of this vacation as a new, rockin' start to your love life. Think of all the possibilities, man."

Nathan glanced at his friend. "Yep. There are plenty of painting possibilities and time to relax." He lowered the window, letting in the warm air from outside. "It's a vacation, like you said. That means something different to me than you."

George grimaced. "Yeah. But try to leave the door open for the beauties on the island."

"I am. That's why I've got my brush and paints with me."

George rolled his eyes. "You know what I meant."

He nodded. "And you know what I meant."

"I give up. You play around with your easel, and I'll play around with live people of the female persuasion."

Nathan grinned, then leaned an elbow on the open window ledge. "Good. You finally see a clash of colors can create an extraordinary canvas."

George gave him a sideways glance, his mouth twisting into a smirk. "Whatever, dude."

He tapped his palm on the window frame. Yes. This trip would be filled with creativity and a fresh start to his life, making new positive memories and leaving the negative ones behind.

Chapter Two

Saturday afternoon, Christina rolled her luggage into the Athens hotel room as Becky opened the window facing the busy street below them. Christina came alongside her friend and peered out. A large, gold-domed church sat at the end of the road. The Spanish-style tiled roof finished off the beauty of its Byzantine architecture.

Christina grabbed her purse. "Want to take a stroll with me down to the church on the corner?"

Becky drummed her fingers on the windowsill. "Nope. I'm not the one interested in church architecture."

"I like all kinds of art."

"Yeah, I know, but you have a thing about churches, and I don't. Knock yourself out."

Becky's distaste of anything having to do with temples was the result of too many forced Sunday services every week and attending a Catholic school growing up. Nobody pushed Becky into anything. Her parents had had their hands full.

Christina chuckled under her breath. The total opposite had happened in her childhood. Her parents hadn't forced her to go to the local Greek Orthodox cathedral, but they did attend often, and she'd always felt at home in that hallowed space where heaven and earth met.

Christina headed to the door. "See you later."

She stepped onto the sidewalk, heat rising from its surface. The summer sun bore down on her. Swarms of people moved past her as if they were a human train, their voices buzzing and snapping in the hot, thick air. The delicious aroma of souvlaki floated under her nose as she strode toward the towering church with its edifice made of red and ecru bricks. Its two wide-open mahogany front doors beckoned her.

Christina entered the narthex. Icons of various saints filled the four blue walls. Lit tapers rose from a sea of sand within a rectangular candle stand. A handful of people wandered the area, and more gathered inside the magnificent nave with its white marble iconostasis and gold-and-crystal chandeliers dangling from the lofty ceiling.

Chanters in their black robes were intoning Vespers. She only understood a word here and there. Her mother had never taught her or her younger brother much Greek when they were children. Her father, who was an American, had thought at the time that learning another language would have been too difficult for them. A part of her wished her mother hadn't listened to him and had taught her anyway.

Christina gravitated toward the candles, fumbling through her purse for money. Next to the stand, she dropped a couple of euro coins into the slit on top of a box. Picking up a candle, she lit it and stuck it in the sand. She crossed herself and headed into the nave, looking up at the domed ceiling with Christ in its center, His right hand blessing her.

Around her, numerous tourists intertwined with a spatter of old, stooped *yiayias* in their black dresses and scarves. Two young nuns stood next to them. Her heart swelled. She could picture herself in a monastery. Her farce of a marriage and embarrassing divorce meant nothing now, only sweet allegiance to the true and faithful Man—Jesus Christ. He'd never hurt her.

Yes, she'd keep an eye out for monasteries and churches to visit while in Greece. It would be a good introduction and warm-up to what she hoped lay ahead.

Caught up in the melodic voices of the chanters, she jumped when a hand squeezed her shoulder.

Becky appeared by her side. When had she shown up?

"I'm starving. Ready for dinner?"

Christina nodded, crossed herself, then trailed Becky out of the church.

THE FOLLOWING AFTERNOON, CHRISTINA STROLLED ALONGSIDE BECKY out of the ferry, pulling her rolling luggage onto the cement dock. The huge, rocky cliffs of Santorini with clusters of whitewashed buildings twinkled in the sun. A salty breeze brushed strands of her long hair off her shoulder. The mass of people surrounding her fanned across the harbor.

Becky pointed to a taxi parked by the travel agency adjacent to the rising rocks. "That's ours."

Christina hurried with her friend to the car and got in.

"Hello, ladies. Welcome to beautiful Santorini," the cab driver said with a toothy grin. Sweat glistened on his wide forehead, his brown hair plastered against his head. Worry beads hung from the rearview mirror. Greek music streamed at a low hum from the radio.

He drove them up the narrow, winding road toward the top of the caldera.

Christina gazed out the open window, the briny wind refreshing against her face.

Reaching the town of Thira, he continued driving through, past dazzling store windows crammed with shiny souvenirs. Music spilled from boisterous restaurants while herds of people strolled the alabaster sidewalks and a few rode rumbling mopeds. Pink and red bougainvillea tumbled down second-story ivory buildings and balconies, the sweet scent of them swirling in the breeze.

All of the landscape was familiar to Christina. Her heart leaped at the sights as she remembered being here with her parents after graduating from high school. Her life had been a clean canvas then, waiting to be brushed and colored with the hues of promising endeavors. That narrow path toward monasticism lay tucked inside her heart ever since two nuns had visited her family's church for a Great Lent retreat on the importance of the Jesus Prayer.

Christina put on her sunglasses against the white sun blazing in the cloudless, azure sky.

"Man, it sure is incredible here," Becky said, wiping her damp forehead.

"As always." Christina gathered up her hair and clipped it in a twisted roll against her head. She took a tissue from her purse and mopped the back of her neck.

Becky nudged her. "Not all of us have been to Greece before, smarty-pants." She blew a huge bubble near Christina's face.

Christina poked the blob with her index finger, and it deflated into a sagging ball on Becky's chin.

"You can't resist doing that, can you?"

"Nope. Too tempting." Christina grinned. "Maybe give your jaw a break and ditch the gum for a while."

"Never." Becky used the chewed wad from her mouth against her chin to clean up the sticky mess.

Christina focused on the blue-domed churches peeking above and in between the collection of buildings. Perfect to sketch and tour. Maybe meet a priest or, if she got really lucky, an abbess. She'd have to check her phone for monasteries on the island. There had to be at least a couple.

The cab stopped in the town of Oia in front of a hotel half wedged into the charcoal-colored cliff. A swimming pool jutted over its edge. The clean white edifice matched the images she'd seen online.

"We here. Hotel Aphrodite." The driver climbed out of the vehicle and gestured toward the double doors to the lodging.

They grabbed their luggage, tipped the man, and headed for the hotel's entrance.

Coolness from the air conditioner swept over Christina as she dug through her purse for her reservations and walked across the lobby floor. Looking up, two men were in her path. She stopped right before colliding with the sable-haired man. She caught her breath. He had a sexy five-o'clock shadow and the most beautiful blue eyes resembling the color of the Aegean Sea she'd ever seen. A fresh, spicy scent—a mixture of citrus and muskiness—wafted under her nose. Her knees weakened, and she struggled to regain her strength, tensing her body in response.

He halted in front of her with his hands up. "Whoa. Sorry about that."

He stood several inches taller than her, his fit, athletic figure donned in cargo shorts and a plain blue T-shirt that hugged his firm chest and stomach. His sandals resembled what an Apostle would wear. A large black duffel bag hung from his shoulder. "I should've been watching where I was going."

She shook her head. "No, I should have instead of staring at my purse." She let out a nervous giggle. Mortified by her reaction, she touched her flaming cheek and frowned.

Becky was already at the counter and looked at Christina with an amused smile. She wiggled her brows up and down. Christina rolled her eyes.

The man gave her a curt smile that revealed adorable dimples. "Please excuse us," he said and moved with his large, stocky friend to the elevators.

Christina pressed a hand to her chest. Her heart was beating faster than it should have been. What was wrong with her? She'd sworn off men, and the first one she ran into on the island, she'd lost her senses. Her hand fisted against her breasts as she ground her teeth. She wouldn't be stupid again. A good-looking man couldn't be trusted and meant nothing but danger.

She marched over to Becky and drummed her fingers on the counter, keeping her eyes on the nerdy clerk while waiting to check in.

Becky scrunched up her face and planted her hands on her hips. "What's with the sour look?"

Christina forced a smile. "Who's sour?"

"You are." Becky tilted her head to the side. "Looks like you're ready to murder someone."

Christina laughed. "You're a loon."

"Just as long as I'm not your victim, I'm fine with you going on a mad, murdering rampage."

Christina chuckled as Becky gave the clerk their reservation number.

"Don't think I didn't notice your reaction to the hunk." She mimicked a dog panting. "Just like one of Pavlov's dogs."

Warmth flooded Christina's cheeks. "I don't know what you mean."

"Yeah, right." Becky guffawed. "No woman would've noticed the gorgeous guy and you rounding second base in the middle of the lobby."

Christina's frustration rose in heated waves through her. "There are plenty of gorgeous guys walking the planet. I don't care."

"Sure. You keep telling yourself that." Becky blew another bubble.

Christina snatched the key card from the clerk, whose eyes widened. "Let's get to our hotel room, okay?"

"Right behind you."

Stepping into the elevator, she inhaled a faint spicy male scent —his scent. She shook herself before turning into a spongy Twinkie. *Ditz!*

Christina scrolled through her phone for churches on the island, keeping her focus on what mattered, while Becky pressed the second-floor button.

Chapter Three

"That was a close one, Nate." George snorted. "Nearly hooked up with a hottie right in the middle of the lobby."

Nathan tossed his duffel bag on one of the beds in their hotel room. "It was an accident."

"Yeah, but did you see the chick's face? Totally captivated. You could reel her in pretty easy."

Nathan gritted his teeth. He wasn't in the mood for George's obsessive references to scoring with every woman he thought was a looker. Nathan had dated enough women to know a lot of them were into themselves or wanting him to be their perpetual entertainment escort. But none as horrible as his last girlfriend had been—a female tornado that had ripped apart his heart. He doubted the raven-haired beauty with the liquid black eyes in the lobby would be any different.

"You've got the looks, brother, and you don't even try." George grunted a laugh.

He clamped a hand on the nape of his neck. Yeah. That was part of his problem. He'd never thought he was good-looking, but women seemed to think so. They couldn't see past his appearance and into the deeper part of his being. It had been nothing but trouble since high school.

George patted his back. "Don't look so glum. People got it way worse than you. You're lucky." George frowned and dropped onto the bed next to Nathan's.

Nathan put a hand on George's meaty shoulder. "Don't sell yourself short, Moose. You've got a lot to offer a woman."

George looked at him with a furrowed brow. Then his face brightened. "You're right." He raised an arm and showed off his huge bicep. "Women can't resist this."

"No. And you've got the Superman look. Every woman sees you as her savior."

George's grin widened. He stood up and went to the window that faced the Aegean Sea below. "Can't wait to go to the beach, man. Check out all the ladies." He turned from the window and pointed at Nathan. "Maybe one of 'em will want a free massage."

Nathan shook his head. His friend was losing brain cells. "We're professionals. Can't use that to lure in women."

"You're right. That was dumb." George paced the floor with hands on hips. "When do you wanna get some grub?"

"It's nearly five. Still early."

"What do you wanna do in the meantime?"

Nathan opened his bag and eyed his pochade box and wet canvas carrying case. "There were a lot of incredible lookouts we passed coming up here. It'd be great to go to one, set up my easel, and paint the view."

"Paint now?" George rolled his eyes and folded his arms across his bulky chest. "Really?"

"Why not? It's the perfect time of day to take advantage of the light and shadows."

George shook his head, then waved a hand. "You go and make your masterpiece. I'm going to the beach."

"Sounds good to me." Nathan grabbed his pochade and wet canvas tote and headed to the door. "See you later."

NATHAN SETTLED ON THE GRASS AMONG RAINBOW-COLORED wildflowers and took in the view ahead of him. The orange sun hovered over the horizon, its tangerine and violet rays a palette of beauty across the indigo sky. The sea breeze carried the chatter of tourists trekking the street several yards away, overlapping the quiet space around him. He inhaled the flowers' sweet scents.

Nathan opened the pochade box, set a canvas on the mini easel attached to the container, and began dabbing tubes of colors onto his palette. He picked out a broad brush and dipped it in a cerulean hue. He raised his hand and gazed toward the scene in front of him but paused as a woman about thirty feet away was sitting by one of the rocky ledges, her shapely legs dangling over the side. Her long, dark hair flowed down her red cotton blouse and ended just above her blue shorts. Small leather sandals lay next to her. She was the woman he nearly collided with at the hotel's lobby. She leaned a notebook on her lap, held a pencil, and began to mark the page with clipped movements.

He followed her gaze to a white chapel on the hill about fifty feet to her right. An ivory stone path snaked its way up to the little church's ivory front door. She continued to stare at it, then down at her paper, presumably drawing.

Was she a professional artist, or was it a hobby like his? Either way, he stifled his curiosity and directed his attention to the blank canvas in front of him, waiting to be covered in hues of the ocean.

He cleaned off the broad brush with a cloth and set it aside. Picking up a thinner brush, he dipped the tip in black paint and began to make short, sweeping strokes across the white cloth. His focus was back on her, and his hand automatically created lines of her likeness on the canvas. It was like he couldn't stop brushing, sweeping, dotting colors that transformed into her. He kept at it, breathless, until the painted image became a vivid replica of her, nearly pulsating off the surface. He cleaned his brush and went back to the thicker one, filling in large portions of the space with streaks of undulating, blue water below her toes.

When he'd finished, he set the painting in the wet canvas case to let it dry.

He cleaned off his brushes, then grabbed a fresh canvas. He set it on his mini easel and concentrated on the landscape before him. But it was as if he'd lost all desire to continue.

She was standing now and walked toward the chapel, her svelte figure moving as if in rhythm with the waves of the sea.

He shook his head, trying to calm his racing heart. *Ridiculous.* He was being ridiculous. So she was beautiful. Yeah? No different from the women he'd dated in the past. All of them had broken up with him for their own selfish reasons. They'd blamed him for being too distracted by his artwork. He hadn't made time for them. Why didn't he know how to have fun... *real* fun? And how did that *fun* end up? Not fun at all. Especially Jennifer. She'd berated him nonstop about her needs. He grimaced. Why hadn't she cared about his needs?

Nathan gathered his art supplies, returning them to the pochade box. He rose from the lookout and walked to the street, not glancing back.

NATHAN ENTERED HIS EMPTY HOTEL ROOM, DROPPED HIS ART BAG ON his bed, and pulled out the painting of the mysterious raven-haired woman. His stomach clenched. Why had he created this painting? *Impulse.* That was all it had been. Something beautiful to brush across his canvas. He paced the floor, scowling. *Stupid.* He was being stupid. What was the matter with him? He stopped near the bed and studied the woman colored in ebony, peach, and stunning red. It was just art. Just beauty. That was all. But his stomach hadn't unknotted, and his heart tightened.

Closing the wooden box with the portrait, he opened the wardrobe, shoved it in the bottom corner, then slammed the door shut.

Nathan dropped into a chair near the door to the balcony. He ran his hands through his hair, clutching onto bunches of the strands halfway through. The hurt from his past relationship still stabbed at his heart. Lost life. Lost love. Believing in something that had never been real. He squeezed his eyes shut, pushing aside the memories of the auburn-haired woman who'd walked out of his life five months ago.

He rose and went to the balcony, the turquoise sea sparkling in the distance. He pictured his past with Jennifer swept away on the waves, a mixture of relief and grief rolling away with them.

Nathan straightened his posture and scanned the white buildings on the cliffs. He was there to spend time with his friend and uncle and create scenes that didn't include women, except the special portrait he'd be making for his grandfather—a portrait of a beloved woman worth remembering.

Chapter Four

Christina traipsed up the alabaster path to the church. She'd managed to make a decent sketch of the little white chapel and would fill in the penciled picture with watercolors later.

Candlelight flickered in the two large windows facing her as she approached the door. Before she could knock, the door opened, and an elderly man with a long gray beard stood in the doorway. A *kalimavkion*, or circular black hat, rested on his white-haired head, and he wore a flowing black cassock. He greeted her with a welcoming smile.

"*Kalispera*." He bowed to her, then held out his right hand.

Christina cupped her hands below his wrinkly one and kissed his. "*Kalispera*, Father. Do you speak English?"

"A little bit."

"I'm sorry to bother you, but I just arrived here this afternoon, and I had to come visit your lovely church."

"*Naí*. Please come in." He moved back and gestured for her to enter. "No service tonight for people. Only a lone monk's prayers." He chuckled.

She hesitated on the threshold. "Oh. I don't want to interrupt your private prayers."

"It not happen until midnight."

"Oh, okay."

"You come here on vacation?"

"Yes."

She stepped inside the narthex where a tiny candle stand stood. The cozy nave ahead of her held a wood-carved iconostasis with hanging vigil lamps twinkling in the dimly lit room. Only the kandelias and tapers lit the room, and it gave her a strong sense of all-encompassing sacredness. The faint scent of rosewater incense wafted in the air. This was what she needed. Peace while here. And maybe in the near future, she'd step out of this world and enter a holy one.

"Please take your time to pray and venerate icons." The monk shuffled to the arched opening to the altar and removed his hat.

She lit a candle and kissed the icons of Christ and His saints in the narthex and nave, then remained quiet while the monk prostrated several times. She found herself copying his moves, imagining herself as a nun—her long hair rolled in a bun and hidden under her head covering.

The archaic space, along with the sweet incense transported her to an ancient world when people had been stronger, bolder in their beliefs. She closed her eyes. Did she have the fortitude to take the monastic vows? Truly live the rest of her life as a nun dedicated to serving God? She scrunched her nose. Doubts from the evil one. She opened her eyes and scanned the small room. *Stop questioning what you know is right for you. You've been drawn to this since you were eighteen. Forget about the stupid marriage and divorce that had veered you from what you're meant to be.* The signs to move in this direction had been with her for years. She couldn't and wouldn't ignore them.

The monk turned toward her, and she bowed. "Thank you for allowing me to visit."

He bobbed his head. "God bless."

Christina smiled and walked out of the chapel. The sun had set, and the sky had turned a darker blue with a sliver of light on the horizon. Tomorrow she'd go visit a women's monastery and track down the abbess.

As she strolled the sidewalk back to her hotel, passing knots of people laughing and eating ice cream cones, she spied blue-eyed amulets hanging from jewelry trees in one of the shop windows. The man she'd nearly crashed into in the hotel lobby came to mind. Those bluer-than-the-sky eyes had locked with her own for just a moment, and a firecracker sparked inside her, heating her whole body. She rubbed her arms, reliving the experience.

The high-pitched melody of a bouzouki floated out of a restaurant, waking her from her thoughts. She shook her head. What was wrong with her? She'd just come from a holy chapel with the monastic life filling her head. She didn't want a repeat disastrous performance in the world of romance.

Still, the guy's dimpled smile and penetrating gaze overran the images of church in her head. Wiles of the enemy, trying to tempt her away from her chosen path, to cause her more pain.

Christina nodded, picked up her pace, and pushed open the doors to her hotel. Blowing out a breath, she straightened her posture and walked through the lobby toward the elevators. Whatever activities she and Becky did tomorrow, they would include a trip to a monastery.

CHRISTINA RUSHED OVER TO THE TABLE WHERE BECKY SAT WAITING AT their hotel's rooftop restaurant. A gyro lay on a plate across from Becky and her plate of chicken souvlaki and rice. Two *lemonadas* stood by their dishes. Her friend always knew what to order for her.

"Geez. I'd been kidding earlier, but I don't know if you caught that." Becky leaned forward with eyes narrowed. "Did you really end up going on a murder tear? Burying the victims?" She shrugged. "I mean, you were gone forever."

Christina rolled her eyes. "You should've known where I was."

Becky screwed up her face in thought before it went lax. "Oh. The church obsession."

"It's not an obsession."

"It became one six months ago."

"There's nothing wrong with wanting to visit beautiful churches."

Becky shifted in her chair. "Nope. There isn't, but you've got to be stepping inside those places for other reasons besides that."

Christina hadn't yet shared her monastic ideas with Becky. She hadn't with anyone. A part of her didn't want to mention it for fear of jinxing herself. She didn't want to announce anything until she'd learned more.

"Not gonna tell me, are you?" Becky pulled a piece of chicken off a skewer and popped it into her mouth.

"Not yet." Christina clasped her hands together in front of her. "Please give me some time."

Becky shrugged again. "I may be impatient about getting to places on time, but you know I've never pushed you on personal issues."

"You're right."

"You planning to show up at another church tomorrow?"

"Um. Yes."

"Just as long as it isn't between two and four o'clock. Remember, we're eating lunch at the Athena Delights restaurant down the street from here."

She'd nearly forgotten. "Oh right."

Becky scooped up rice on her fork and shoved it into her mouth.

Christina took a bite of her sandwich, the flavor of the grilled lamb and beef filling her mouth. She swallowed the delectable food and smiled. "I wonder if the food is as good there as it is here."

"I'm thinking every restaurant on this island has amazing

food. But I hope it has some live music or something. Adds spice to the dining experience, leaving no chance for boredom."

"I'm sure it at least has music."

"Of course, if there are some hot guys there, boredom and I may never meet." Becky winked and pointed her hand in the shape of a gun at Christina.

Christina chuckled. "I know for certain *you* are never a bore."

"I'm not only here for a shoulder to cry on but to entertain, maybe juggle a few apricots tomorrow at one of the markets in town. Jackie of all trades."

Christina finished her gyro, then grinned. "Your talents are endless."

"You better believe it." Becky pushed her empty plate away. "Ready to go?"

"Yeah."

She signaled the waiter, then they strolled out of the restaurant.

They entered the elevator, and Christina pushed their floor number. The doors opened a minute later, and they walked down the hall to their room.

"While you're snooping around churches, I'll be burrowing my feet in the sand at the beach, enjoying a delicious, cold drink under an umbrella." Becky swayed her hips in exaggeration with a hand hovering by the back of her head, as if she were strutting down the catwalk.

Christina giggled. "Your second home."

"I was born in water."

"Yes, you've shared the story a million times about your mom giving birth to you in a pool."

"I'm part mermaid." Becky flashed a big grin.

"The way you swim, no doubt."

"Having been on the high school swim team didn't hurt either."

"No, definitely not."

"You were too caught up in drawing still life to dive into pools then."

Christina draped an arm around Becky. "My love of drawing has never died out."

"Yep. And you're pretty good at it."

"It's relaxing."

"Just like floating on your back in water."

The man and his friend Christina had run into earlier in the day came out of the elevator, moved to the second door down, and disappeared inside their room.

"Ooooo. Those two cuties are on the same floor as us." Becky bumped her hip into Christina's.

"Yeah." She steadied her legs that had morphed into Jell-O, then used her keycard to unlock their door.

Becky craned her neck, her attention still focused on the men's door.

Christina pulled Becky by her arm into the room, and the door clunked shut. "Tomorrow. The beach, remember?"

"You bet."

Christina searched her suitcase for her toiletries and night shirt. A warm shower would wash away any wasteful, random thoughts that weren't part of her set plans. Maybe even scrub away the last dark memories of her marriage and divorce.

Chapter Five

Midmorning, Nathan trekked through the alabaster archways and white stone paths in the quaint village of Pyrgos. He'd just left a tiny shop where he'd purchased a porcelain dish with a bas relief of Santorini, its white-and-blue buildings expertly painted.

He leaned against the wall of one of the covered passageways, sheltered by the sun's hot rays. Quietness whispered through the area.

Ahead of him, modest ivory and salmon-colored homes boasted two-foot, solid white walls serving as fences. Perched on top of these short barriers were rotund terra-cotta pots that held vibrant pink, red, and purple flowers spreading like colorful umbrellas over them.

The silence and beauty surrounding him emoted a kind of sacredness, as if he were passing through an outdoor church, the floral aroma adding to the sense of reverence.

His mind filled with endless scenes he could capture on canvas.

The faint shuffle of shoes against the stone pathway came from behind him. He looked over his shoulder. The woman from his hotel with her silky, ebony hair pulled back in a swaying ponytail slowly approached him. She wore a long, multicolored skirt and white blouse that accentuated her perfect figure. She carried a shopping bag. Large round sunglasses veiled those dark, mysterious eyes. Her red lips pursed together as she stopped a few feet from him.

"This time I was watching where I was going," she muttered without a smile. She rolled her shoulders, her hands fidgeting with the strap of her purse.

He caught her vibe. She was nervous. He moved out of the mini tunnel and pressed his back against the wall for her to pass freely. "Sorry for hogging the space. Please go ahead."

"Thank you." She scurried past him, the sweet scent of flowers and tangerines wafting in her wake.

His fist pressed against his thumping chest. Every time he went someplace, she appeared like an apparition. But there was no mistaking she was real. And the electricity running through him told him he was an idiot. Fawning over another beautiful woman. Acting like a panting puppy dog. *Disgusting.*

He'd done his souvenir shopping, and he planned to meet with his uncle at his shop before joining George at the beach for lunch. He pivoted in the opposite direction she'd gone and headed back toward the main street.

CHRISTINA WAITED TO LOOK BACK AT THE STONE TRAIL UNTIL SHE WAS sure the guy from the hotel couldn't spot her. She'd turned to the right, where the path curved up and toward a small courtyard and monastery with its modest ivory-and-cobalt-colored church. She peeked around the corner. He wasn't there. She blew out a breath.

Shaking her head, Christina continued toward the church. No matter where she went, he showed up. Was he stalking her? A chill ran through her. The man was a total stranger. Women had to be careful wandering around alone. But she'd never thought vigilance was necessary on Santorini. She glanced over her shoulder at the empty lane. She'd keep an eye on him and her surroundings from now on.

Christina reached the courtyard and crossed to the church's white doors. The monastery sat high up on the village's rocky elevations. The late-morning sun beat down on her. Thankfully, her blouse and long skirt protected her skin from baking. A slight breeze brushed her face, giving her momentary relief from the heat.

The doors to the chapel and monastery were wide-open, with a sprinkle of sightseers inside the church. Unfortunately, for the past thirty years, the convent and church had been used as no more than museums.

She entered the church, where all the interest seemed to be. The coolness from the shaded foyer washed over her sticky skin. She inhaled the scent of fresh paint and dusty stone. People murmured around her, taking pictures with their phones and pointing at the frescos on two of the nave's walls. The murals depicted scenes from Christ's life.

Christina scanned the round interior for any clergy. An older woman looking to be in her fifties, wearing a full-length black robe and head covering—the type an abbess would wear—stood by the candle stand. *Aha.* She'd found the nun she'd read about online—the only one on the island. That had to be a sign her pursuit of becoming a nun was heading in the right direction.

She bounced on the balls of her feet, twisted her purse strap with anxious fingers, then approached the nun.

The abbess smiled. "Welcome to Saint Nicholas's church." She pressed a small hand to her chest. "I'm Abbess Angelique."

"Thank you. I'm so glad you speak English." Christina smoothed down her hair, working on how to breach the subject. "I'm Christina, here on vacation."

"Nice to meet you, Christina." The nun chuckled. "I suspected you were a vacationer. Most everybody is."

Christina's laugh came out jittery and embarrassing. Her face warmed. "Of course. You're right." Who else would be coming there when the buildings were museums? She'd have to figure out how to change the vacationer conversation into an interest in monasticism.

"Were you wanting to take a tour of the old monastery and the gift shop?"

The kind woman had just given her a great segue for her questions on being a nun. "Oh, that would be fantastic." She glanced around, realizing the monastery may not do individual tours. "When does the group tour start?"

Mother Angelique shook her head. "We don't get enough visitors for group tours. We take whoever is interested when they come to visit us."

Christina reached out her hand toward the abbess. "Oh, I'm sorry to hear that." How sad the abbess didn't get many visitors. Not even with the buildings now museums.

"Not to worry. God provides for what little we need here."

Christina nodded. "Can we start the tour now?"

"Certainly." The abbess led her out of the tourist-filled church to the attached chalk-colored building and gestured her toward the open entryway.

Christina moved into the spacious room with a sitting area and bookshelf on the left and a gift shop on the right.

"This is where we serve sweets to our guests." She pointed at a table with a dish of Greek braided sugar cookies. "Please help yourself."

Christina picked up two. "Thank you."

Next to the dish rested a woven bowl with paper money and coins inside. Christina dug in her purse, pulled out a few euro bills, and set them in the bowl.

"Thank you." Mother Angelique beamed, then waved a hand toward the shop. "We sell our prayer ropes, books, icons, and the like here."

Christina nodded. She had a feeling the tour was going to be short, considering the only other place to wander was down the narrow hallway past the gift shop.

The nun turned in that direction.

She touched the woman's robed arm. "I was wondering if you could help me."

"That's what I'm here for."

"I would like to become a nun, and I need to know how to go about starting the process."

The abbess took Christina's hand in hers and patted it. "There are many steps, but first, have you gotten the blessing from your spiritual father to pursue this calling?"

Christina bit her lip. The last news she'd shared with her parish priest, Father Michael, was wanting to attend his adult education classes Wednesday evenings. She'd come out of hiding a couple of months ago, after the divorce was final. She'd been embarrassed to show her face, knowing the whole parish, including Father Michael, knew about her divorce.

Frowning, she shook her head.

Mother Angeliqué laid a gentle hand on her shoulder. "It is okay. It is not hard to approach your beloved spiritual father to discuss your noble pursuit toward monasticism. He can help guide you toward what you need to do."

When would that be? Would she race to the church when she returned from vacation and pour out all her desires to Father Michael then and there? What would he say?

"But while you're on vacation, you can visit a monastery. It is always a blessing to do so." The abbess tilted her head to the side. "I'm afraid there aren't any women's monasteries on the island. But you could go to Aegina and visit Saint Macrina's Monastery. It's very active, and they receive many inquirers and pilgrims."

Images of happy nuns singing in their church and working together in their garden floated in Christina's head. Yes. She could do that and bring up her experience to Father Michael. That could be a great opening in receiving his advice on her future endeavors. She smiled as her muscles tightened with pent-up anticipation. "That sounds wonderful." She'd get a ferry ride to Aegina before she left the island for the mainland.

"Our galley kitchen is at the end of the hall if you wish to see it."

"Sure."

When the tour ended, Christina headed down the alabaster pathway toward Oia and her hotel. The information about Saint Macrina's Monastery on the island of Aegina could be another sign she was meant to be a nun. The doors kept opening for her to move in that direction. Maybe her meeting with Father Michael would go smoothly with all these developments.

Would she tell Becky her plans to visit the monastery now or wait until closer to the time they'd be leaving Santorini? She tapped a finger to her chin. She'd wait. Then Becky wouldn't have time to talk her out of it. She continued down the stone passageway.

Chapter Six

Nathan approached his uncle's shop, its name, Sea Treasures, scrawled in navy blue across a white wooden plank hanging above the door. Several groups of people loitered in front of the store's big window, chatting and gawking at the many artistic items, including paintings of boats and harbors, sculptures of fish and other undersea life, smooth, colorful vases, and unique jewelry.

He entered the store and spied his uncle at the front counter. *Thío* Ioannis was dressed in a beige linen suit and a white shirt. His brown eyes, large and intelligent, twinkled behind black-rimmed glasses, and his chin sported a goatee. His uncle's skin was tanned—how he'd always remembered him. He'd never seen the man without one. Then again, his uncle loved to go fishing, and that afforded him a lot of time to soak up the sun's rays.

A memory surfaced in Nathan's mind of *Thío* Ioannis standing at the harbor, asking him many times to go fishing with him, but the deep, unpredictable water had always come between him and his uncle's time on his boat. If only he hadn't been such a pigheaded ass when he was a kid, refusing his parents' prodding for him to take swimming lessons, maybe he'd have thrown out the reel next to his uncle.

"Nathan, my boy!" *Thío* Ioannis came around the counter, spread his arms, his mouth stretched into a wide smile.

He hugged his uncle, and they exchanged kisses on the cheeks. "It's great to see you, Uncle."

"You too." *Thío* Ioannis patted Nathan's shoulder. "Oh." He pointed toward one of the bare walls from where merchandise and shelves had been pushed away. "Come, let me show you."

Nathan followed his uncle to the area.

Thío Ioannis gestured with a wave of his arm. "This is one of the walls we will work on. Then..." He crooked a hand and moved to an arched opening to another smaller room.

Nathan entered after his uncle.

"Then we work in here. My office." *Thío* Ioannis held up two fingers. "Two walls we will paint in here." He grinned and lifted his arms, as if showcasing his office. "You ready to work soon?"

Nathan took in the twelve-by-twelve-square-foot space, his spirits lifting at the thought of what he would create on those two walls and the one in the shop. A split second of nervousness slid through his stomach, not wanting to disappoint his uncle if he'd mess up. But he shook off the fear. He'd painted dozens of walls before, and they all turned out better than he'd thought they would have.

He smiled. "I'm ready."

"When you want to start? Tomorrow?"

"Sure. That'd be great."

"Very good." *Thío* Ioannis gathered Nathan in his arms again. "You come by tomorrow around seven in the morning, and we work for two hours before the shop opens." He let Nathan go. "How's that?"

"I'll be here."

"Ah." *Thío* Ioannis chuckled and slapped Nathan on the back. "I must go back to work now. See you tomorrow morning."

Nathan waved and headed out of his uncle's shop, his mind swirling with ideas of colorful sea life murals.

NATHAN SPOTTED GEORGE SITTING ON A LOUNGE CHAIR NEXT TO A blonde who looked as if she needed a sandwich. Her collarbone protruded in an unflattering manner, and he could count the ribs below her skimpy bikini top. George howled as if he'd won big at a slot machine, as the woman giggled and ran a bony hand through his thick brown hair.

He moved toward them with hesitancy, not wanting to break up their flirt fest. The blonde with her raccoon eyes and puckered pink lips spotted him before George and tapped George's arm just as he reached them.

"Hey, Nate." George glanced at the bag in his hand. "Did you see your uncle?"

"Yes." Nathan shifted from one foot to the other. "Did you want me to head back to the hotel without you?"

George's stare traveled from him to the woman now leaning back in her chaise, eyes closed. He patted her hand. "I've got to talk with my bud for a while. Okay?"

The woman shrugged and grinned. "Go ahead."

George beamed before leaving his seat and guiding Nathan to a couple of beach chairs near a restaurant's back patio.

Nathan sat and set his bag on the sandy ground.

George plopped down next to him. He smacked the metal arm of the chair. "Did you see that beauty?"

Nathan glanced back at the skinny woman now lying on her stomach. "Yeah."

"Ran into her at the bar inside there." George jerked a thumb behind him toward the restaurant. "She struck up a conversation like we'd known each other forever. It was freaking amazing."

"What'd I say?" Nathan smiled. "Women love Superman."

"You were so right. Man, this vacation is gonna be stellar. Soon I'll be up to my eyeballs in X chromosomes."

Nathan laughed and turned his attention to the waves rolling onto the shore a few yards away from them. His hands clutched the arms of his chair. There was no way to know when that water dropped off into a deep, inescapable trench. He'd heard from a couple of friends back home in Santa Fe how they'd taken vacations to the Pacific coast, ventured into its cold water, and ended up sinking under the murky surface after taking no more than a dozen steps.

His own frightening experience with a local lake had stayed with him since he was eight years old. He'd been throwing rocks into the lake, slipped on one of the larger stones, and fell into its murky water. He remembered the panic that had seized his body, making him go rigid. His father had fished him out. He staved off a chill. He'd never learned to swim, and since that incident, he had been too scared to go near water again. His refusal to learn the life skill came back to haunt him once again. *Damn.* He wouldn't be such a wimp now if he hadn't been one then.

George nudged his arm. "I looked up boat tours here. Thought we'd go out Sunday afternoon. Take a look at the rocks and fish."

His grip tightened. "I don't know…"

"Come on. You don't have to jump in the water. Just sit in the boat and take in the view." George swatted the air and leaned back in his chair. "We came here to do fun things, not sit around and paint."

"Painting this island was one of the reasons I came here. It's a perfect place for it."

"Yeah, yeah, but not all freaking day."

"I don't paint all day."

"The tour is a couple of hours." George slapped Nathan on the back. "You can manage that, right? You're a big boy."

Nathan tore his gaze from the waves that seemed to have grown in size. "Yeah." He ground his teeth. "No need to treat me like a toddler, Moose. I'll go, of course. But with a life jacket."

"Well, duh."

Nathan sighed and reclined in his chair.

"So, I'll call later to set up a reservation for around one or two. May be able to pick up a couple of ladies before then to join us."

"Sure." No longer listening to George, Nathan ran a hand through his hair and wished he were on one of the rocky cliffs painting instead of a few feet from the roaring sea.

Chapter Seven

Nathan squeezed in between people pouring into Athena Delights restaurant, the space alive with laughter, chatter, and thumping tunes coming through four recessed wall speakers situated around the room. Painted Greek mythological figures covered the walls. People packed the dozens of tables. A group of patrons had merged two long tables together. They were singing something in Greek to a middle-aged man at one end of the table, probably celebrating his name day.

George gestured for him to follow. They headed to where other diners had spilled onto the open patio. Every table was occupied by at least four people, except one, where the two women from their hotel sat.

Nathan wasn't about to approach them. He didn't need another curt exchange with the dark-haired beauty. He jerked a thumb in the direction they'd just come. "There're plenty of other restaurants in town. I'm sure we can find one that isn't half as full as this one."

George jutted his chin toward the two women. "Hey, the two hot chicks from our hotel. Maybe they'll let us join them."

Nathan stiffened, suddenly warm. He tugged on the collar of his shirt as the warmth crept down his neck. Must have been from all the bodies crammed in and outside the building. That had to be it. There was no way he'd gotten that flustered over the woman he'd nearly run into in Pyrgos. "Bad idea."

"Great idea." George strutted toward their table, glancing over his shoulder. "Perfect way to get to know them."

Nathan sighed and trailed behind George. The man could never drop his *women-are-in-the-vicinity* detector.

When they were a foot away from the women, they looked up at him and George.

"Hello," the redhead said with a clipped wave. "Aren't you guys staying at the same hotel as us?"

George grinned so wide Nathan expected his friend's wisdom teeth to appear.

"We sure are," George said. "Hey, we Americans should stick together, right?" He laughed.

The redhead tipped her head back and joined George's nonsensical jubilance. The raven-haired woman looked as if she wanted to crawl under the table. Her beautiful lips curved into an unnatural, forced smile, and her ebony stare bounced back and forth from her friend to her lap. This wasn't good.

Before anyone could say anything else, George pulled out the chair next to the redhead and made himself at home, as if they were long-lost friends. The man had courage or gall, depending on the opinion of the person upon whom he imposed himself.

The redhead gestured for Nathan to take the other empty seat, which was too close to the fidgeting Aphrodite. "Sit down, sit down."

He slowly sat, keeping his focus on the table. The heat radiating between him and the dark-haired beauty was nearly unbearable. And her floral, citrusy scent teased his nostrils. What kind of wicked influence did this woman possess? He turned his head away from her and inhaled twice to center himself. Again, he was getting caught up in the woman's aura... or whatever it was.

"I'm Becky," the redhead said, then pointed at her friend. "And this is my best friend, Christina."

Christina. Of course. Her name was as gorgeous as she was. He stifled a shake of his head and peered at her from his peripheral. She was creating strange designs with her cloth napkin.

She didn't look any more comfortable than he, so what did it matter? He was there to simply eat lunch, not slip a ring on her finger and deposit her in a "Just Got Married" car. *Idiot.* All he had to do was eat his food and enjoy the restaurant's artistic and musical atmosphere. Nothing wrong with that. Nothing at all.

"I'm George, and this is Nathan," his friend said with a lifting of his chin and prideful smile.

"Good to meet you," Becky said and jabbed Christina in her side.

Christina grimaced, leaning away from her friend. "Yes."

The waiter showed up, setting down baskets of bread, four small plates, and four waters. They ordered entrées of calamari, salads, gyros, fries, and plenty of wine and beer. It was three o'clock, after all.

"So, where you from?" George asked.

"Colorado Springs," Becky said.

"Awesome place."

"We think so." Becky grinned. "Where do you hail from?"

"Santa Fe."

Becky leaned her forearms on the table. "Wow. You aren't that far from us."

"Pretty cool, huh?"

"Yeah."

As George and Becky gabbed on, Nathan glanced at Christina. Might as well try to do the same. "What brought you to Santorini?"

She looked at him with an intense stare. He didn't know exactly what the stare meant, but his heart sped up anyway. His body betrayed him every time.

"A needed vacation, like most people."

He let her retort fall away. "Same for George and me." He cleared his throat while smoothing out the tablecloth, pushing himself to continue talking. "What do you do back in the Springs?"

She pressed those luscious lips together, as if he'd asked her an offensive question. But a second later, she displayed a weak smile. Did his question embarrass her? What the hell did she do for a living?

"I'm an administrative assistant at a small benefits consultant company."

How was that an embarrassing career? He didn't know but didn't dwell on it. Maybe she was just nervous about having an uninvited stranger join her for lunch. He nodded. "Sounds like a great job."

Christina gave him a tight smile. "I like it. Pays well enough."

"That's helpful."

"Yes." She took a sip of water. "What do you do?"

"My friend and I own a massage center. We are licensed massage therapists."

Her face went pink, and she was back to producing odd shapes with her napkin. "That must be nice... owning your own business."

"The seven years since we've opened the place have been amazing. Lots of returning clients."

"I'm sure," she muttered just loud enough for him to hear her. She grabbed a piece of bread and crammed it into her lovely mouth. Not the most gracious move, but he didn't care.

The stunning earlier image of her in the white passageway came back to him. "Pyrgos is a nice little village. Did you have a good time exploring it?"

She set the last half of her uneaten bread on the small plate in front of her. She locked her gaze with his, her face serious, a slight furrow in her brow. "Yes, I did. What were you doing there?"

"Got a few souvenirs at the town's shops."

She actually laughed. "Well, that's good. Means you weren't stalking me."

He froze. "Stalking you?"

"You seem to be everywhere I am, and since I don't know you... A woman can never be too careful."

He shifted in his chair as irritation rose inside him. She didn't know him. If she had, she'd never have made such a comment. He calmed himself by smoothing down his hair. Yeah. She didn't know him at all. But still, did he look like a stalker? He didn't think so. What the hell did stalkers look like anyway? Women came to him. He didn't have to seek them out. But he wouldn't boast over that, reminding himself of his dismal track record.

"Are you going to answer me?" she asked, her expression still teetering on harsh.

He brushed off her critical remark. "No, of course I'm not stalking you. I don't stalk women, or anyone, for that matter."

The waiter arrived with their meals, and he concentrated on his fried squid, listening to George and Becky still conversing.

"I was captain of my high school swim team," George bragged, puffing out his bulky chest.

Becky raised her brows and gaped. "No." She held up a fist and grinned. "I was my swim team's lead too."

"Sweet." George bumped fists with Becky's.

They certainly seemed to be hitting it off. But that was how it usually went with George and women. He had something that attracted women to him. Probably his affable good-naturedness. Nobody could ever call him a quiet introvert, like Nathan thought of himself.

He and Christina remained quiet throughout lunch. The tension between them had him draining his mug of beer and pouring another. She nursed her glass of wine.

Hoops, hollers, and clapping started up, and groups of people at tables near their own abandoned them and formed a line. They began to clumsily dance Greek style, obviously many of them tourists. An olive-skinned man with two other men appeared at the entryway to the inside of the restaurant and joined the line of dancers.

"Want to give it a whirl?" Becky rose from her chair and held out a hand toward George.

George barreled out of his chair, nearly knocking it over. He steadied it, then followed Becky to the end of the human chain.

Nathan wiped his mouth with his napkin and stole a glance at Christina. She was watching their friends stumbling about, laughing as if they'd drunk too much. But they hadn't, especially George. With a tank for a body, he could consume large quantities of liquor, and on certain occasions, he did. Nathan didn't take in as much as George and not as often either, but sometimes it was nice to let go.

He put his bundled napkin on the table. *What the hell? Why not ask?* "Do you want to join in the fun?"

She shook her head, her cheeks pink again. "Oh no. You go ahead. I've got to get going. There are some things I need to do." She got up from her chair, just as he did.

He'd expected her response, but he smiled when she looked his way.

"Nice meeting you," he said, jamming his hands into his shorts pockets.

"You too." She grabbed her purse and whisked over to her friend before escaping through the entryway to the restaurant's dining room. Did she think he was going to stalk her even though he'd told her he didn't do that creepy stuff? He wasn't an asshole.

He grunted and sat back down to finish his beer.

Chapter Eight

Christina stopped outside her hotel, out of breath. She looked over her shoulder. He hadn't followed her. Maybe he'd told the truth—he wasn't stalking her. Her hands trembled, her body was warm, and her heartbeat pulsed in her ears. If he hadn't followed her, what was she afraid of?

She fisted her hands, tapped them on the sides of her head, and paced the sidewalk. *Dummy*. The man was a woman magnet. Just looking into those pools of blue eyes took everything she had not to melt or, worse, crawl into his lap. She knocked on her head again. He kept messing up her plans. A nuisance, distraction. She'd gotten oodles of signs the life of a nun was in her future. Not another gorgeous, conceited, cagey man. *But he hadn't come off as conceited or cagey...* She stomped her foot. *Stop it*. She wouldn't continue to wallow in thoughts of him.

Down the street, a large, illumined church beckoned her. She jogged over to it and stepped inside its cool narthex. Her breath evened out as she glanced around the space devoid of tourists.

An ancient priest with his hand on a cane, sitting in a wooden chair near the entrance to the nave, grinned at her with two missing teeth. He said something in Greek.

She smiled back. "Hello. I'm sorry. I don't know much Greek. Do you speak English?"

"*Naí*. My English." He wiggled his hand side to side. "It is *étsi ki étsi*."

She approached him with cupped hands. He lifted his right hand, blessing her, before she kissed it.

"There are no services right now."

"I just wanted to come and look."

He gave her an abbreviated bow. "My child, you came here for more than that."

She tensed. His English had improved remarkably. "What do you mean?"

He waved an unsteady hand. "It is not for me to answer."

"But you brought it up, Father."

"Yes. Forgive me." He gazed at her with childlike eyes.

She wrung her hands. An urge came over her to tell him her plans. Maybe he could help guide her until she could talk to Father Michael back home. "I did come here for something more." She paced the marble floor. "I came for some peace." The heated encounter at the restaurant niggled at her. She stopped moving. "Lunch was… unsettling."

"Your heart also."

She paused, putting a hand to her chest. She nodded, moved toward him, and kneeled. "You see, Father. I want to become a nun."

"*Naí*."

"I talked to an abbess today, who told me to visit Saint Macrina's Monastery on the island of Aegina."

He remained silent.

"It was wonderful to find an abbess here, and so I'll be going to Aegina on my way back to the mainland in a few weeks."

The elder still said nothing.

"Do you think that's a good idea? Going to Aegina, I mean."

He tilted his head slightly to the side, giving her a look that said "It's possible," but he didn't speak.

She smiled as images of the conversation with the nun came to her mind. "I can't wait to go."

He held up a shaky finger. "Are you truly certain you desire to take that path?"

She stood. "Well, yes. It's been a plan of mine since I was eighteen."

He nodded.

"And that's the life I want. I *need*."

"Perhaps you should work out the troubles within your heart first."

Her mouth fell open as chills ran up her spine. How did he know what was in her heart?

"One rarely knows what one needs when one's soul is darkened with anger, hurt, self-pity, pride. It's best to meditate on one's motivations and do, as they say, a self-reflection before making any such momentous life decisions."

Christina backed into the candle stand, her body stiff, her mind churning.

The old priest lifted a feeble hand again. "Do not worry. Take time in your decision. God bless you, my child."

He leaned on his cane and labored to rise from the chair. She rushed over and helped him stand.

"*Efcharistó*." He pointed at the door. "I must go and rest now before evening prayers." He plodded out the door, and she followed him. He pulled out a key from his cassock and locked the church door.

She clasped her hands together. "Thank you, Father."

"You're welcome." He blessed her and trudged down the sidewalk, his cane clacking against the stones.

Christina strode back to her hotel and headed to her room. Once inside, she stripped off her clothes and shimmied into her one-piece black bathing suit. Three vanilla-scented candles sat on a desk by her bed, and she lit them. She then walked to the balcony, opened the door, then dipped her foot in the pool's cool water. She needed this after the intense lunch encounter and the experiences with the nun and priest. Too much to take in. Slipping into the five-foot-deep pool, she leaned her head back and dunked her hair, the water refreshing. She breathed in and out with her eyes closed, the water massaging her body. The tension released from her.

The elder knew what was in her heart without having ever met her before. She'd heard about such clairvoyant clergy, especially through the stories of the saints. Never had she imagined running into one on a tourist island, of all places.

She leaned her forearms on the edge of the pool, facing the stunning caldera, the sea of alabaster buildings nestled in the rocky landscape with the turquoise water below her. A cruise ship glided along the calming waves. The late-afternoon sun spread peach hues across the sky.

Of course, she'd take the wise priest's advice and look inside herself and sort out all the wreckage that had happened with Justin. After all, the elder didn't say she shouldn't pursue the monastic life. He'd left the door open, giving the advice most priests gave—examining her decision and heart. She could and would do that. She took the ancient clergyman's advice as positive, and she added the encounter as a possible sign leading on the track toward becoming a nun. After all, why would she have run into this precious old man if not to help her toward a pure and good goal in her life? Still, this priest wasn't her spiritual father. She would have to obey Father Michael. She grimaced. What would Father Michael say?

In her world, there was no such thing as coincidence. Because of that belief, her run-ins with Nathan also weren't coincidences. But how he fit into the picture was unclear to her. She sighed and leaned her chin on her hands. This vacation was turning out to be much more than sunbathing, shopping, and admiring pretty churches.

Chapter Nine

Nathan arrived at his uncle's shop right on time. The CLOSED sign dangled on the door. He turned the knob and found it unlocked. He entered tentatively, and not seeing *Thío* Ioannis behind the counter, headed past the empty space to the office.

Thío Ioannis was setting out the art equipment for his job when he stepped into the room.

His uncle, kneeling next to a box of supplies, twisted at the waist and looked back at him. "Ah, right on time, my boy."

Nathan grinned. "Didn't want to be late for my first day on the job."

"Very good." *Thío* Ioannis let out a gravelly laugh and rose. He straightened out his shirt and shorts, then pointed to a small closet. "There are smocks in there to save your nice clothes."

Nathan took out an apron and put it on while his uncle headed to the entryway.

"I would like you to start in the shop since that's what most of my customers will see first."

"Got it." Nathan carried a gallon of blue paint, a box of paintbrushes, and smaller containers of hues to the wall in the store.

He set the items down and gazed at the white wall. Sea

creatures, water, and a blazing sun penetrating the calm water ran like a kaleidoscope through his mind. After opening the gallon of paint, he grabbed a wide roller and pan. He began the process of covering the white wall with brilliant blue, vertical section by section, getting lost in the scene both in his head and the blue water he was creating with every roll. He would run another coat over it soon.

The boat ride George had mentioned to him yesterday and eagerly scheduled for Sunday had Nathan sighing and sitting on the hard, white-tiled floor. What a dichotomy. Painting the Aegean and dreading being on a boat in less than a week. He could have said no to George, but that would've been wrong. He came with George to do tourist things with him. Maybe the peace he got from painting this big mural would warm him up to the boat trip. He glanced at the white-and-blue wall. He could almost believe it.

"You gonna add a fishing boat to your painting, right?" His uncle appeared next to him with a wide grin.

Fishing boat. He hadn't thought of that, even after thinking about the boat tour. He glanced at his uncle. "Sure, *Thío.* I can definitely add it."

"Good, because..." His uncle made a sweep of his arm, showcasing the items and the name of the store. "It's what this is all about. What *I'm* all about." He chuckled and slapped Nathan on the back.

Nathan laughed and held up a hand. "I know, I know."

Thío Ioannis bent and loudly whispered in his ear even though nobody was in the shop. "I still wish all the time you come fishing with me."

Nathan froze, his heart tightening. This had always been a huge deal to his uncle. He frowned, feeling helpless about what to say.

Thío Ioannis squeezed his shoulder. "No worry. It'll happen when it is right time."

His uncle gave him a kind smile. He turned and, with a slight slump in his shoulders, walked back to his office.

I'm hurting him, hurting his feelings. Nathan pressed a fist to his thigh. He needed to do something about this phobia, if not for his sake, for his uncle's.

CHRISTINA LAY BACK ON A LOUNGE CHAIR, SOAKING UP THE afternoon sun with Becky in an identical position next to her.

"You ran off at lunch, and then you were asleep when I came back to the hotel. I never got to tell you about the fun I had with George last night," Becky said, raising her head to look at Christina before resting it back against her chair.

Nathan's big, rowdy friend. How could she forget? He'd had no problem inviting himself and Nathan to sit at their table. Being a lover of old, black-and-white movies, Christina found the two friends opposites, like Abbott and Costello—a funny duo from 1940s films. She laughed under her breath.

Becky swiveled her head toward her with a puckered face.

She gave her friend an apologetic smile. "Sorry. What happened?"

"We hit it off." Snapping her gum, Becky sat up in her yellow one-piece bathing suit that enhanced her fire-engine-red hair. "He's so easy to talk to. In fact, he never runs out of things to say. A natural gabber. Real winner." She flexed an arm. "And did you see the guns on him? He could easily sweep me off my feet to the moon for all I care."

"Wow. You're really taken by him."

"Yep."

"When are you getting together?"

"Oh, honey, this is the good part." Becky nudged Christina's arm. "Guess what?"

"What?"

"He loves to swim and snorkel."

Christina leaned on her elbows. "Are you going to go snorkeling with him?"

"Of course. But let me get to the juicy part that has to do with both of us. He invited us to go with him and his buddy on a boat tour Sunday afternoon. Can you believe it? What luck."

Christina's stomach fluttered. Together on a boat with no place to escape but into the Aegean. Too small a space for all four of them. Actually, it would have been too small a space if it had been just her and Nathan. She rubbed her stomach.

"Yeah, I know you kicked Nathan to the curb yesterday even though you guys had barely gotten to know each other."

Before Christina could defend herself, Becky held up a hand.

"Don't think I didn't catch the body language between the two of you." She shook her head with lips pressed together. "I might not have caught most of what you guys said, but the expressions said everything, especially yours."

"What? What expressions did I give?"

"Let's just say, if you had superpowers in those coal-black eyes of yours, you would have sliced him in two by the glares you gave him when he wasn't looking your way."

Christina sat up. "Come on. You're exaggerating. I didn't feel like slicing him in half, for crying out loud." Maybe she would have wanted to stuff him in a locked room to keep a wall between them. But that was all. He was a constant distraction, and her body and heart didn't always obey her mind.

"Sure." Becky rolled her eyes, then leaned the palms of her hands against the lounge chair. "Anyway, I already told George we'd love to go."

Christina gaped. "But you didn't even ask me."

"You were asleep. Not my fault." She smiled in her friendly way. "Besides, we had no other plans."

"You don't know—"

"You'll have to cancel the next church you wanted to scurry off to for that day, if you'd planned that far ahead. It's all set, and they're counting on us being there. At least I know George is. And it's only for two hours. You can handle that."

Christina gripped the lounge chairs' arms as she tried to steady her trembling body. She had to get ahold of herself and quit freaking out over everything regarding men. A simple boat tour for a couple of hours wouldn't kill her. This was a vacation. There were bound to be boat trips, swims, sunbathing, lots of meals in restaurants, and more shopping to do. She rolled her shoulders. Yes. She could do this. No problem.

"All right."

"Fabulous." Becky blew a bubble, then smiled.

NATHAN ENTERED ONE OF THE SHOPS IN OIA WITH GEORGE BEHIND him. The building's white walls were covered in posters, paintings, and sculptures. Shelves filled with ceramics and vases took up half the store while racks of women's and men's T-shirts and other clothes took up the other portion of the building. A glass counter of jewelry, blue-eyed amulets, and worry beads stood near the clothes. The table next to it held small baskets of prayer ropes and bracelets, as well as saint icon pins and various clip crosses to attach to car visors and blazer lapels. Greek pop music streamed through the place.

George headed to the T-shirt racks and Nathan toward the worry beads. They hung from a jewelry tree. One made of polished dark wood caught his attention. They were perfect for his grandfather. He remembered Papou rubbing them and clasping them in his hand as he talked to his friends while drinking coffee on his back patio. Papou would drape the string of beads over the rearview mirror in his car and take Nathan to the park, mini golf course, or the outdoor theater. They'd swing gently to the rhythm of the lively music his grandfather would play throughout the drive.

Nathan removed the beads from the tree and smelled them,

the scent a mixture of rosewood and cedar. He smiled as his fingers held one bead at a time.

"Nathan Galanis," a woman's voice called from behind him.

He turned around and faced a woman with shoulder-length, golden-brown hair, brown eyes, long nose, and oval face. She wore plain blue shorts and an orange top on her modestly shaped figure. Her mouth widened into a grin. She looked familiar, but he wasn't sure where he'd seen her.

She approached him with open arms. "Nathan, my old childhood friend." She embraced him with a gentle squeeze.

Images of a young girl running with him around the playground, collecting seashells on the shore, and eating watermelon at his grandparents' house came back to him. He smiled and hugged her. "Thalia. I can't believe it's you. It's been so many years."

She let him go and looked at him. "You grown very tall." She used her hand to measure their heights. "You are six feet, no?"

"You're right." He chuckled and pointed at her. "You've grown too." He leaned against the counter. "I didn't know you had family on the island."

"I do not. It is a small two-week vacation from my home in Athens."

"When did you get here?"

"One day ago. I come here to rest."

"I don't blame you. It's a perfect place for relaxing."

Thalia nodded, then studied the merchandise on the glass counter. She picked up one of the cross clips and snapped it on the scooped neckline of her top, then removed it. She shook her head. "It better for car."

He picked up another clip, turned it back and forth, then put it back. "Yep."

She pointed at the worry beads in his other hand. "They beautiful. You get?"

"For my papou."

"Papou Petros." She smiled. "I miss him."

"I'm sure he misses you too."

George lumbered over to them. "Hey." He looked from Thalia to Nathan.

"George, this is my good friend Thalia. We met each other back when I'd come to see my grandfather during summer vacations."

George grinned and put out a hand that Thalia shook. "Nice to meet you."

"And you." She flashed him a smile and grabbed a black prayer bracelet.

George elbowed Nathan and leaned toward his ear. "Why don't you invite her on our boat tour?"

Nathan glanced at Thalia as she slipped the bracelet on her skinny wrist. She'd been like a sister he'd never had. Last night, George had told him he'd invited Becky and Christina to the boat excursion. He hadn't been happy but not really surprised by George's impulsive behavior. That was George. But having Thalia on the boat would be a great buffer and hopefully a distractor from Christina. "Thalia, would you like to come with us on a boat ride Sunday afternoon at one?"

Her mouth formed an O before spreading into another sweet smile. "That would be great. Thanks very much."

"It's my pleasure."

"You want to walk around, catch up a bit after leaving the store?"

"Sure."

George saluted Nathan, then headed toward the register with his large blue T-shirt that had the words ISLAND HOPPER across it in white letters with a picture of the caldera below it.

Nathan trailed him with Thalia by his side. After they paid for their items, they left the store and hit the sidewalk, the brightness of the sun making the buildings sparkle and mists of steam float up from the street. What luck to have run into Thalia, his cherished childhood friend. Maybe they'd collect seashells later for old time's sake.

Chapter Ten

After lunch on the shore with Becky, Christina headed to the lookout where the tiny chapel she'd visited last time sat several feet above the overhang. She'd brought her drawing notebook and pencil to create a sketch of the beautiful caldera.

A strong wind swept over her as she approached the cliff. She stopped abruptly, and her muscles tensed. Two figures, a man and a woman, sat on the ledge, their backs to her. Even from behind, Christina could tell the man was Nathan, his short, wavy sable hair fluttering in the breeze.

Who was the woman? She'd never seen Nathan with anyone but George. Jealousy nibbled at her, and she fidgeted with irritation. Why be jealous? The man could date whomever he liked. He wasn't hers, and she belonged to no one. That was the way she wanted it.

Nathan turned to his right to face the woman next to him.

Christina pivoted, looking behind her, then toward the chapel. Could she make it back to the street and hide behind one of the buildings before he saw her, or was it quicker to race to the chapel to hole up? She judged the distance, and the chapel won out. She sprinted up the stone path toward it, not daring to look back, and hurried through the open front doors. Nobody was inside the building.

She pressed a hand against her chest, waiting for her heart to slow to a regular rhythm. She blew out a breath. Nathan probably didn't see her. He was too wrapped up talking to that woman. Jealousy crept in again, but she pushed it aside. Gazing at the iconostasis, she crossed herself, but curiosity urged her to peek out the window. Stepping gingerly to the side of the window, she peered out. Nathan and the woman were still there, but from her vantage point, their faces were visible. The woman's body was less curvy than hers but longer. The strong sea breeze splayed the woman's light brown hair across her face.

She gripped her notebook in her left hand and pencil in her other. Could she still sketch the landscape to the right of her, or was the scene obscured? She glanced in the direction of the caldera. The angle allowed her, if she wished, to draw a narrow snapshot of the scenery. Without thinking, she flipped open the sketchbook and turned her focus on Nathan. Her hand moved the pencil across the sheet, using thick lines for his strong jaw, sweeping curves for his hair, a careful sketch of his straight, perfect nose, and gentle, detailed shading and light strokes for his beautiful eyes. If only she'd brought her colored pencils. She'd have colored them in with the brilliant azure pencil.

Why was she breathing hard? Drawing had never been a laborious activity. Christina bit her lip while working on his tanned body, with its toned arm muscles showing just below his short-sleeved green T-shirt. She'd have to fill in the colors back at the hotel. She sketched the cliff he sat on, then looked back toward her subject.

Nathan and the woman were now standing. The woman turned toward the street. Nathan swung partially around, and his gaze traveled to the chapel, to the window in which she was in full view.

Gasping, she slid over and pressed her back against the wall. Had he seen her? Her heart thudded like horse's hooves galloping inside her. She hugged the notebook to her chest, closing her eyes. *Calm down.* The chapel was at least fifty feet away. There was no way he'd have been able to spot her, especially with no lights other than the flickering candles in the vigil lamps hanging in front of the iconostasis.

She looked out the window again. Nathan and the woman were already on the sidewalk, walking toward the many shops.

Christina crossed herself, then exited the church.

She stood where Nathan and the woman had been a few minutes ago, as the wind blew through her hair and against her body. The brunette with Nathan wouldn't leave her thoughts. Her fists clenched. She was going to be a nun. Who cared about some woman with Nathan? Who cared what Nathan did? She certainly didn't.

Christina kept repeating this mantra to herself, hoping the words and feelings would finally sink in, as she headed for her hotel.

"IT WAS GREAT CATCHING UP, THALIA," NATHAN SAID OUTSIDE THE shop they'd been in earlier. "I'll see you maybe tomorrow?"

Thalia waved. "Yes." She walked toward the next store ahead.

Nathan spotted George and Becky approaching him from down the street.

"Hey, Nate. Your friend gone?" George asked when they reached him.

"Yes."

George's hand joined Becky's, and he looked down at her, grinning like a lovestruck teenager. "Becky and me, we're going to the beach for a while."

"Have fun. See you later." Nathan made his way toward his hotel.

He stopped at the intersection of the sidewalk and the dirt path that went in the direction of the lookout. Earlier, out of the corner of his eye, he'd caught sight of Christina running to the little church as if her ass were on fire. He shook his head. Did she actually still think he was after her? With Thalia there? And he'd seen her spying on him through the church's window. Who was stalking whom? Hmm.

Nathan reached the hotel and headed to his room. Inside, he took a seat on the balcony, with the turquoise sea below. The strong breeze had created unsettling waves. He hoped the wind wouldn't be this out of control during Sunday's boat ride. He'd have to take Dramamine before getting on the craft. His jaw tightened as his body tensed. He'd need to get a grip on this boat tour. He couldn't show his fear of water. They'd think him a coward. He tapped the arm of his chair with a palm. All he had to do was sit on the boat and avoid examining how deep the water was around him. Look relaxed. He could do that. He had to do that for two hours on that damn boat. But two hours wasn't forever. He could handle it...

Chapter Eleven

Christina sat at the desk, tore off the sheet from her sketching notebook, and added watercolors to her drawing of Nathan. Concentrating on his facial features, she was careful to just add a dab of blue hue to his eyes. She worked on the colors of his clothes, then brushed with gentle strokes his strong, perfectly shaped legs, his skin a glorious bronze color, which she managed to pull off by mixing yellow and brown together. She finished off the sea and bright sun in the partly cloudy sky and added the effects of a breeze to the scene, giving an almost dreamy look to Nathan and his surroundings.

She pushed the paper to her left and got up from the chair, her heart racing. She jerked a glance in the painting's direction, clamping both hands behind her neck. Painting always sucked her into the colored canvas, swallowed her whole, living in the image she'd created.

Why did she sketch Nathan? She paced the room, blowing hair from her forehead. She'd specifically gone to the outlook to paint the caldera. She folded her arms across her chest, her mouth firm. It was as if she'd had no control at that moment, gripped by a strong impulse to draw him. She dropped into the chair again. *What's wrong with me?*

Christina raked a hand through her hair over and over again, trying to temper the frustration and irritation simmering in her. She glanced at the paper once more, as it continued to dry. She should throw it away. Why keep it?

She shot from the chair, reached for the sheet, but paused before touching it. Her hand shook. She couldn't do it. She couldn't tear it up, throw it away.

"Ugh!" She knocked her knuckles against the sides of her head, then pointed at the image. "If I can't destroy you, then after you're dry, I'm stowing you out of sight."

Fifteen minutes later, Christina slipped it on one of the shelves in the wardrobe and shut the door with a click. She licked her lips and nodded. "Okay. It's all good."

She checked her watch. Nearly six o'clock. She'd grab something to eat, then visit the church down the street again.

On her way to the church, Christina spotted a woman and a man heading toward her. As they got closer, recognition hit. She gasped and ran toward the woman.

"Maria!" Christina shrieked, holding her cousin tightly.

"Cousin." Maria drew back and gave Christina a wide smile. "Surprise!"

"Mom must have told Aunt Tula I was here."

"Bingo." Maria gestured toward the man next to her. "But we already had this vacation booked. Great timing, eh?"

"Very." Christina laughed. "How long are you going to be on the island?"

"Till Sunday morning. I'm here with my friend Dino."

The dark-haired man had a thick beard of matching color, and his small brown eyes danced. Towering over her and Maria, he must have been six feet five. His height and bulky body looked like he could have been a former linebacker.

"Nice to meet you," Christina said with a nod.

"You too."

"We're headed to Dino's friend's restaurant and bar now. Where are you going?"

She pointed at the church. "I'm going to go check out that church."

"You going to paint it?"

Christina swung her head left and right while gripping her purse. *Crap.* Her art bag was back at the hotel. She was becoming absentminded on the subjects she'd originally planned to paint when she'd come to the island. She squeezed her purse's strap, irritated with herself. "Well, no. I forgot my stuff. But I'll get a good look inside and will definitely return tomorrow with my supplies."

"Enjoy the tour, and we'll see you around." Maria kissed Christina's cheeks, then walked off with Dino in the opposite direction.

"Okay," she called after them, walking backward toward the church.

She noticed Dino look back twice at her before Maria smacked his arm and pulled him along. Christina rolled her eyes. *Men.*

The wind had died down to a whisper as she entered the magnificent edifice. The same elderly priest sat in the wooden chair with his cane resting against one of his cassock-covered, knobby knees.

He lifted a trembling hand and smiled. "Ah, my child, you've come back."

She bent and kissed his right hand, and he blessed her. "Yes, Father." She gazed around the narthex. "I love this place."

He nodded.

"Is there a service tonight?"

"*Naí.* Paraklesis."

"Great. Is it starting soon?"

The priest glanced at an old-fashioned, wind-up watch on his bony wrist.

They still make those old wind-up watches? Wow.

"About half an hour."

"Okay. I'll just wait then."

He nodded once more, leaning his wrinkled hands on his cane.

She paced the marble floor, happy to be wearing flats. The elder pulled a small book from the folds of his robe and opened it. His mouth moved with eyes lowered to the words.

Christina wrung her hands and stopped pacing, feeling she was interrupting his reading or praying. She lit a candle, then moved into the nave to give him privacy. She sat on one of the chairs in the second-to-last row of the hallowed space. The silence brought her comfort, and she soaked it in with her eyes closed.

She then checked her phone. Ten minutes had gone by. She looked over her shoulder toward the narthex. He wasn't there. Where had he gone? Maybe he needed to use the bathroom or went to a quiet area in some hidden room to pray.

Curiosity brought her back to the narthex with the single light of the candle in the sand, shedding a faint glow in the area. A door on the left was closed, and a staircase next to it probably led to the balcony above the narthex. She crept up the wooden stairs to the shadowed loft and gazed down at the lines of chairs and the marble iconostasis straight ahead. The chandeliers dangled from the ceiling, equal to her eye level. She scanned the surrounding seats, but the elder wasn't there.

Christina headed back down the stairs to the narthex. Curiosity still nipping at her, she gripped the doorknob of the closed door and turned it, but it was locked. Maybe he left and would return when the service started. She stepped outside where people crowded the sidewalks. A handful of them entered the church.

There was no sign of the priest. But he'd have to return for the service. She tilted her head to the side. Why? He didn't say he was staying for the service. But he was a priest. He was supposed to be at the services. He was old, though, and probably wasn't the priest who did the services at this church, she reasoned with herself.

She pivoted back to the entryway into the church. The priest was sitting in the wooden chair. She caught her breath and hurried toward him.

"Father, where did you go? I was looking all over for you."

He bowed his head and smiled. "There are many children who need guidance and comfort."

He'd gone off to counsel someone in just ten or fifteen minutes? Christina wrinkled her nose. There was no way.

"You have not come to a peaceful resolution," he said. "You have not yet discerned what is the right path."

She froze, then kneeled next to him while the few tourists who had entered the building earlier wandered the nave. Only she and the elder were in the narthex. The wide double-doored entry let in purple and pink shafts of the sunset, its crown peeking over the tops of the buildings. Despite the many people swarming the street, buzzing with chatter, it sounded as if she had been transported to another time, the noises muted, and only she and the elder were there.

Again, he knew what was in her heart and mind and most likely her soul. She swallowed and gazed up at his frail, wrinkled face, his brown eyes twinkling like that of a young boy.

"Yes, Father. I'm still working out my path." She shook her head. "I'm not sure why. All the signs—"

He patted her hands clasped together on her knees. "You know you must converse with your spiritual father all that is in your heart, and he will help lead you on the path toward God." He held up a finger. "There is more than one path."

Which meant marriage or monasticism in her... *their* world. But she'd tried the marriage route, and it had been a total failure.

"Keep your eyes on Christ and continue on your journey." He gestured toward a middle-aged, rotund priest passing them, entering the sanctuary, and strolling toward the altar. "And come to services when you are able, even on your holiday." He grinned widely, showing the two gaps in his row of teeth.

"I will. Thank you, Father." Christina rose and helped the elder stand.

He hobbled into the nave as she watched from the narthex, biting her lip.

A warm scent of wood and citrus wafted under her nose just before Nathan passed her and lit a candle. Her heart sped up, and she took a step back. There he was again.

His stare locked with hers, showing something akin to sadness. A small smile brightened his tanned face, a hint of his dimples showing.

Butterflies chased each other in her stomach. She took hold of the candle stand, her knees weak.

"Excuse me." He went inside the nave, crossing himself.

Christina's mouth fell open. *He's Orthodox too.*

He stood in one of the middle sections on the right side of the sanctuary as two chanters walked by Christina and headed to the podium also on the right side of the building.

Soon the chanting of hymns to the Theotokos started. Even with all the beautiful words within those songs to the Mother of God, Christina couldn't stop stealing glimpses of Nathan, who faced the altar, standing attentively.

When the service was just about to end, she slipped out of the church, her heart filled with too much emotion, warmth, and joy, mixed with consternation. She ran toward her hotel. The streetlamps and shops' windows spread rich yellow light on swaths of the white-tiled sidewalk and dark asphalt of the street like a lit trail.

In her hotel room, Christina crossed to the balcony. Opening the door wide, she inhaled the briny sea air and exhaled, dropping into a chair next to the pool. Had Nathan's appearance been a sign toward a different path? The elder wouldn't have given her any other indications of what lay ahead of her. He would expect her to figure out her plans with her spiritual father and God's help.

She stood and leaned her elbows on the balcony's ledge,

gazing out over the cluttered buildings and rolling Aegean Sea. Images of Justin and the loss within her flooded her mind. She squeezed her eyes shut and shook her head. "No. I'm not going to wallow in the past."

The door to the room opened, and Becky sauntered in, popping her gum. She grinned. "Hey, Christina. What you been up to? Church hopping?"

Becky's face fell as she approached Christina. "What happened?"

Christina fought off tears. "Bad memories, that's all."

"He's history, been history for over a year."

Christina pressed a hand to her stomach. "I know. But it still hurts."

Becky put a hand over Christina's. "That hurt will stay with you longer than that two-timing prick."

Christina bit her quivering lip and nodded.

Her friend led her back into the room and had her sit on the bed.

"What brought this on? Surely not church. That's your happy place, so you say."

"I met a sweet old priest in the church down the street. Actually, tonight was the second time I've run into him."

"Okay." Becky chewed her gum quietly as she swept Christina's long strands of hair off the shoulder closest to her.

"He's clairvoyant."

"Hmm."

"He didn't tell me anything about what my future is or anything like that."

"Sounds more solid then, to me."

"It's just, when I'm around him, all my past mistakes and future plans mesh together into a ball of chaos and uncertainty."

Becky pursed her lips. "Not a very helpful priest."

Christina shook her head. "No. It's not him. It's me. I'm still a mess."

"Still pining over that ferret?"

"No. What I want to do with my life."

Becky leaned back, her hands on her thighs. "I don't see how charting out all the possibilities you have going for you equates to a mess. I mean, really. You're twenty-seven, beautiful, kind, a little stubborn, a picky eater, and when you get involved in something, you're like the proverbial dog with a bone—"

Christina planted a hand on her hip and narrowed her eyes at her friend. "Were you trying to make a point?"

"Oh. Sorry. Yeah." Becky blew a bubble. It popped, and she sucked it back into her mouth, nodding. "You've got your whole life ahead of you. Don't narrow down your choices." She held up her hand as if grasping for something toward the sky. "Reach for the moon."

"I don't want the moon."

Becky's brows knitted. "Well, I sure as hell don't know what you want. You've been a whirlpool of moodiness for months now. I can't help you if you don't tell me what you want."

Christina's heart twisted. Nathan's face floated in her head, followed by the elder's, then images of her in a nun's habit in a monastery somewhere. She leaned her elbows on her knees and pressed her palms against the sides of her head. "I don't know what I want."

"Well, that helps a whole lot."

Christina frowned at Becky.

Her friend's face brightened with one of her amiable smiles. "You worry too much, girl." She stood before Christina and waved her arms around. "We're on vacation on a beautiful island."

Christina sighed and, once more, inhaled the sea air gently drifting into the room from the balcony. "You're right."

"This is a time to relax, enjoy not having work or anything to fuss about. A time-out from the regular dregs of life." Becky popped another bubble. "Let yourself go... let go of trying to control everything and allow what's to come, come. It's how to live life. How to live it without Xanax and Ambien."

Christina chuckled, and the chuckle turned into a laugh. The laugh grew into stomach-splitting giggling, as she fell back on the bed. Becky flopped on the mattress next to her, laughing along with her.

"That-a-girl. Keeps away the ulcers." Becky snorted.

They fell into another round of laughter.

"Thanks, Beck. You're the best." They sat up, and she hugged Becky.

"I know I am." Becky patted Christina's back. "Now just remember this talk tomorrow." She pulled away and pointed a finger at Christina. "I want to see evidence of you working on letting it go."

Christina bit her lip, then smiled. "I'll give it my best try."

"That's all we can ever give."

Becky headed toward the bathroom. "I'm getting ready to hit the hay. I've got a date with George on the beach for a late breakfast and swim tomorrow."

Christina watched with admiration her friend sashay into the bathroom, wishing she had Becky's free spirit. Maybe someday Becky's optimism would rub off on her.

Chapter Twelve

Nathan gazed with approval at the yellow fishing boat bobbing on the cerulean water he'd created on the wall. It was one of three boats he planned to paint. His uncle would appreciate the extra ones.

"Ah, you've added my favorite thing in this glorious world," *Thío* Ioannis said behind him.

Nathan, squatting, swung around on the balls of his feet, leaning his forearm on his thigh. His uncle wore a tackle hat and held a fishing pole.

"You've been fishing."

"Every morning around six."

"Wow. That's dedication." Nathan chuckled and set his paintbrush on a tin pan.

Thío Ioannis gestured toward the mural. "It's coming along nicely. It will be finished soon, yes?"

Nathan wiggled his hand side to side. "I'm halfway there."

His uncle leaned his fishing pole against the counter and slipped off his hat, tossing it on the countertop. "I must get changed. It is almost nine o'clock—opening time."

Nathan went back to work, dabbing a brush into an orange

hue on a palette and brushed it onto a spot in the water, transforming the ball of orange into a plump fish. He used a thin, pointed brush to add yellow-colored scales to the sea creature.

"Tell me, my boy, you got a young lady back home?"

His uncle had returned in khakis, a white shirt, and sandals.

Nathan paused, lowering his head. Images of Jennifer with her suitcase and backpack walking out the door and slamming it shut rolled through his mind. Her expression had been a mixture of repugnance and pity, and sickness had filled his heart and stomach. Squeezing his eyes shut, he blotted out the horrible memory.

Thío Ioannis's gravelly laugh brought him out of the mire.

"Not going to share your romance with me, eh?"

"Sorry. No, I don't have a girlfriend."

"How old are you now?"

"Twenty-nine."

His uncle raised his head, his mouth opening and spreading into a smile, his gaze toward the ceiling. "I'd already been married to your *Thía* Angie four years by that age."

Nathan grinned. "And she still puts up with you after all these years."

Thío Ioannis laughed and slapped Nathan on the shoulder. "Love will do that to you."

Not always. Nathan frowned.

"My boy, why you look so sad? Woman troubles?"

"I did have some, but that ended a few months ago."

"Then why the long face?"

Nathan looked away, wanting to hide the embarrassing warmth filling his face. "It was rough. Didn't work out well."

"I'm sorry." *Thío* Ioannis squeezed his shoulder. "But you will find the right woman, and it will be the best day of your life, like it was for me."

Doubting his uncle's words, Nathan only nodded, not wanting to cause disagreement. What he'd failed to do those months before was unforgiveable... He didn't see how he'd ever get past it.

He went back to scaling his fish, working to delve himself into his painting and the solace of the scene.

MIDAFTERNOON, CHRISTINA, DONNED IN A FUCHSIA PEASANT TOP, beige shorts, and leather sandals, strolled the sidewalk toward her favorite precipice. Her long hair pulled back in a French braid kept her neck cool. Carrying her sketchbook and pencil, she bent to touch the soft petals of a beautiful hydrangea bush at the corner of a small shop. Continuing forward, bougainvillea spilled from pots in front of stores and tumbled down balconies, their sweet scent floating in the light breeze.

She traipsed through the wildflowers to the outlook and caught sight of Nathan sitting where he'd been yesterday. He had a small easel in front of him, a paint palette, tubes of colors, and brushes. As she drew closer, she studied the canvas that displayed several alabaster buildings at the farthest end of the caldera, a lone windmill's arms extending like matchsticks against the bright yellow of the afternoon sun. He seemed so engrossed, not hearing or noticing her now standing next to him. His hand with the thin brush continued to dot and stroke the cloth with a gentleness and preciseness that impressed Christina. His work was good. Very good. She couldn't help but smile. Amazing art always brought her joy.

She'd taken Becky's advice and was putting "letting go" into practice. Although she realized she was hugging the sketchbook to her chest, her pencil in her right fist. She inhaled and exhaled, working to relieve the tightness in her muscles.

Nathan set down his brush and stared out at the sea. He gave a nod toward his work.

Taking another breath and telling herself it didn't hurt to sit with a fellow artist, Christina lowered herself to the ground, a foot away from him on his right.

He turned his head toward her, his mouth falling open, and surprise flashing through those unbelievable eyes of his. She laughed under her breath.

"Hi." She smoothed the hair on the left side of her head and smiled. "I didn't know you could paint."

He kept staring at her as if in disbelief that she was sitting next to him. He licked his lips and swiveled his head from his painting to her three times before answering. "Yes. It's my hobby, my passion."

He focused on his work again, and she studied his strong, handsome profile. A one-inch scar imprinted the skin above his right brow. She'd never noticed it before. But when had she looked at his features this close up, this intently? Not until now. His stubbled cheek and chin and the scent of him screamed all male. Her stomach danced with butterflies while her heart swelled.

Alarmed by her reaction, her body tensed again. *Calm down. Let go. Let this go wherever it's supposed to go.* She exhaled out the anxiousness, forcing herself to remain sitting.

She set down her pad and pencil, the items nearly sticking to her damp palms. "It's really lovely. Your painting."

He looked at her. "Thanks. I've gotten only half of it done so far."

"You don't mind if I draw alongside you, do you?" Her face warmed as his gaze traveled over her face. She lowered her eyes and busied herself with opening her sketchbook. "I love to draw. And I fill it in with watercolors afterward."

"You paint too?"

She nodded and flipped to older pictures she'd drawn and colored and showed him one of them of the chapel she'd visited yesterday. "See?"

Nathan tilted his head to the side with his mouth open. He

reached for her notebook. She held on to it a little too tightly. *Is he going to think it isn't that good?*

"I'd like to look at it closer, if that's okay," he said.

"Oh sure. Of course." She let go and chuckled, patting her hair again.

He stared at the drawing for a long minute. "This is really good, Christina."

His deep voice saying her name made her body melt. She'd never heard her name sound so perfect.

"Thanks."

He nodded and handed back her sketchbook.

She flipped her book to a blank page while he went back to painting.

As she drew the lines of the horizon ahead of them, she asked, "How long have you been painting?"

"Since I was five. You?"

"Around the same age."

While he was busy in his work, she turned the page and drew his profile in quick strokes and shading. A smile played on her lips as she slashed curved lines across a small portion of the paper for his dark hair.

He kept to his artwork and looked as if he lost himself in his paintings as much as she did in hers. She finished the sketch and turned back to the page with the half-done horizon. When she began to create the cheerful sun, he gestured toward his canvas.

"All done." He grinned, the adorable dimples winking back at her. "What do you think?"

Christina set down her pad and pencil and leaned toward the easel, his cheek only inches from hers. She could hear his breathing, smell his spicy, citrusy cologne, feel the heat of his body. She closed her eyes, centering herself from feeling light-headed and her bones softening into liquid. Forcing her eyes open to examine his picture, the painting was beautiful and mirrored the buildings on the caldera in amazing detail and clarity.

"Wow, Nathan. It's absolutely stunning." She swallowed, and her belly filled with warmth. "You've got a real talent."

She faced him, their eyes meeting, mouths open, her breathing short and raspy.

"Thank you," he said, as his gaze traveled from her eyes to her lips.

A rustling and crunching sound came from behind her.

"Nathan, what you doing here?"

Christina looked over her shoulder at the same moment Nathan did. The woman she'd seen yesterday stood there with arms bouncing against her sides.

"We have lunch together, remember?" The woman's lips pursed as her stare flicked from Nathan to her and back to Nathan.

Nathan gaped. "Oh right." He gathered up his art supplies in the box next to him, wiping off brushes, screwing closed the caps on the tubes, and gently setting the easel and painting into another wooden case next to the box. "I'm sorry. Got caught up in my painting." He gave her an apologetic smile.

Christina closed up her notebook and stood when Nathan did.

The woman kept staring at her, as if she was both confused and irritated by her presence. She slid her arm through his, turning her back on Christina.

Nathan glanced behind him, locking his gaze with hers. "Thanks for sharing your art with me."

Christina nodded with a smile as they walked off, but the smile faded quickly as her heart sank. She didn't want him to go. They were creating art together. And there had been a comfortable silence between them while they were immersed in their work. In unison. There was something so beautiful about it.

The moment when they'd nearly kissed came flooding back to her, her body trembling and tingling from the memory. She blew out a breath. Whatever happened between them was stronger than her and probably him by the looks he gave her. What had this been all about? A sign? Could this be another path? A very different one from a damaging marriage and divorce and the road toward black robes and perpetual head coverings? Or was this just a trick by the enemy to make her stumble off the righteous lane?

She swung around and gazed at the boats bobbing on the sea. Becky might have been right. There were many choices out there. Which one would be hers?

Chapter Thirteen

Christina entered her hotel room and leaned on the door when it clunked shut. She was smiling again. She hadn't smiled this much in months. And her heart fluttered and swelled.

She moved across the room as if there were clouds beneath her feet and went out on the balcony. Setting her notebook on the little table next to the pool, she sat in the chair for a moment, drinking in the view and inhaling the aroma of grilled lamb from the hotel's restaurant above her.

Christina opened the sketchpad to the drawing of Nathan. She'd get lost filling in the picture with watercolors.

Someone knocked on her door. She flipped the sketch of the horizon over Nathan's profile and headed to the door. Must be housekeeping. She scanned the room. They didn't need the sheets changed.

Another rap came at the door. She opened it and nearly fell backward as waves of nausea and light-headedness swept over her.

Justin, with messy, ash-blond hair grinned at her. He appeared all-around scruffy, wearing torn jeans and a white T-shirt with stains from God knew what. "Hey, Tinkerbell. Surprise!"

She cringed at that old, insipid nickname he'd given her six years ago when they'd been dating. He'd called her that, he'd said, because of her sweet smile and perfect figure. Swallowing hard, she tried to find words to answer him.

Before she could, Justin slid past her into the room and surveyed it with hands on his hips. Why was he here? How was he here?

He held up his hands. "Yeah, I know. You're wondering what I'm doing here."

"Of course, and how you got here." Christina folded her arms across her chest, straightening her spine, working to calm her nerves.

"I flew." He snorted.

My God. What had she ever seen in him?

"How did you know I was here? My mom would never have told you."

"You're right there. She's always hated my guts." He laughed and fell back on Becky's bed as if it was his. He lay there with fingers laced together across his chest and a huge grin on his face.

She balled her hands into fists. "Then who told you I was here?"

"Your brother was nice enough to tell me."

Christina backed into the desk chair. "What? Steve wouldn't tell you anything."

"Okay, I lied." He sat up and shrugged. "I begged your dad."

"My dad? He wouldn't—"

Justin slid off the bed and stood in front of her. "Yeah. I told him I was sorry and wanted to make amends. Your dad always wants you to be happy and doesn't believe in divorce, so…"

"So, you lied to my dad to come here to do what?"

He raised his arms as if to pull her into a hug. She dodged him and moved toward the door.

"No. I came to make amends, like I said."

She yanked the door open. "It's too late for that."

"It's never too late."

"We're divorced. You wanted it. Remember?"

"I was an asshole."

"Still are."

He sighed heavily. "I flew all this way and get this from you? Can't you give me some time while I'm here?"

She eyed him. "How long are you planning to stay?"

He shrugged. "As long as it takes."

"That won't be long because it isn't going to take."

Justin frowned and ran a hand through his hair. "I know I made a lot of mistakes. I was hurting."

His words socked her in the stomach. "*You* were hurting?" Christina dropped in the desk chair. "You never recognized my pain and told me to get over it."

"Yeah, see? I wasn't thinking right. I was grieving."

Christina couldn't believe what she was hearing. She rubbed her temples where a dull headache began to pulse. She leaned her elbows on the desk and continued to massage her head, pushing back past hurts.

His hand squeezed her shoulder, and she jerked in her seat from his touch.

"I guess I should've let you know I was here instead of just showing up."

She didn't answer, just closed her eyes and wished he'd go away.

"I'll let you be now. We'll talk tomorrow. I'm in the hotel two buildings down from yours. The Dolphin Inn. This one was all booked up. I'll call you around eleven tomorrow morning."

The swishing of his jeans became fainter before the door clunked shut. She exhaled and leaned her head on her folded arms. All the ugly events of the past hit her like a tsunami, and she wept bitter tears.

THALIA SAT ACROSS FROM NATHAN ON THE PATIO OF A SMALL restaurant. "Who was the woman with you at the lookout?"

Nathan's mind filled with images of Christina. He'd been totally caught off guard by her presence and the fact that she had been actually friendly, kind even. And to make the encounter more unbelievable, they found they had something in common. Art. He smiled. "Christina."

Thalia tilted her head to the side with the sides of her mouth slightly turned down. "Is she your girlfriend?"

He chuckled. *Like that would ever happen.* "No. George and I met her and her friend, Becky, a few nights ago. They're from America too."

"Oh." Thalia tapped her fingers on the table as her face brightened. "That is nice. How did you meet them?"

"I nearly ran into her at our hotel."

"She stay at same hotel as you?"

"Yes."

"What is your hotel name so I can meet you there for Sunday boat trip?"

"It's Hotel Aphrodite, just a couple of blocks down from here."

"Okay. I look forward to boat ride."

The looming boat tour. *Ugh.* He shifted in his seat. *Change the subject.* "Tell me what you've been up to since childhood."

"I finished school and then went to university for business. Now I work at a local travel agency in Athens." She patted the top of his hand with hers. "How about you?"

"Been a massage therapist for the past seven years with my friend and partner, George. We're loving it."

"What a good job to have."

A waiter showed up and took their orders of souvlaki, salads, and sodas.

"The boat trip will be fun, no?" Thalia nodded. "Just three more days."

Nathan's stomach knotted. He sighed and took a sip of water, needing to think of something else so he could digest his food. "Yes... fun. Have you gone to any of the beaches on the island yet?"

"You want go with me tomorrow? We can pick up shells like the old days."

The childhood memories loosened the knot in his belly. He chuckled. "Sounds good. What time?"

"How about—?"

"Oh crap. I can't tomorrow. George and I are hiking most of the day in Fira."

Thalia frowned. "Maybe Saturday?"

"I should have a few hours to spare for an old friend and seashells."

She beamed just as the waiter came with their drinks and salads, setting the plates in front of them. She lifted her glass of soda. *"Kali Orexi."*

Nathan picked his up and clinked his glass with hers.

Chapter Fourteen

Christina threw on a knee-length cotton skirt and a T-shirt. She made sure to leave the hotel and turn off her cell phone before eleven a.m. Justin's sudden appearance still rattled her, and she needed time to figure out what to do about it.

The church's double doors were wide-open as she walked toward them, shaking her head. Justin had messed up her vacation. The whole purpose of the trip was to get away from work and her old life. She'd started a new one with different pursuits. Nathan's gorgeous face came to mind. The special encounter they had yesterday stumped her afterward. She wondered what it all meant. But she wasn't able to mull it over for long. Justin ruined that.

Christina stopped on the sidewalk a few feet away from the doors to the church. And what did his showing up mean to her already confusing future plans? She raised her brows. Did it have to mean something? She scowled. It had to. There was no such thing as coincidence.

Entering the church, Christina instinctively looked to her right, where the old priest often perched. But the seat was empty. Her shoulders slumped. She'd really needed to talk to the elder, get his advice. Things were becoming more and more complicated.

Only a handful of tourists wandered around the nave. She'd slip in to do a few prayers about her situation.

She brushed hair from the side of her face and pivoted toward the candle stand. When she finished lighting a taper, she swung around and found the elder settled in the chair as if he'd been there for hours. Her mouth fell open, and she crossed the few feet of marble to him.

"Father, I didn't see you a few minutes ago."

"My spiritual children needed my guidance."

He'd said that before.

A couple entered the narthex, murmuring in a language she didn't understand, and walked past her and the priest and into the sanctuary as if they weren't there.

She squatted in front of the priest. "Father, I never asked your name, what to call you."

He gave her one of his childlike smiles. "Father Apostolos."

She returned the smile.

"You have come to tell me something?"

"Yes." She sighed and lowered her gaze. "Things have gotten worse."

"You have realized there are many paths to God."

"Yes, and all but one is confusing."

He chuckled. "Have you been praying for guidance?"

She nodded with vigor. "But obstacles keep getting in my way."

"They are there to encourage you to discern and resolve your situation in time."

Her stomach churned. "But I don't know what to do."

He laid a wrinkled hand on hers that clutched the arm of the chair. "Continue praying and interacting with those obstacles. Like the floating fog of a dewy morning, the veil of mist will dissipate, and your decision before you will be as clear as glass."

"But when?"

"You must have patience to find your way to discovery."

The fact that Justin was literally in one of the hotel rooms across from the church didn't help. She got up from the floor and wrung her hands. "That's hard to do..."

"Such decisions of importance are."

Becky's words came back to her. She needed to let go of the worries and keep moving forward with faith that things would work the way they were meant to. She faced the burning candle she'd lit, as she continued to ponder those thoughts.

Three of the tourists in the nave walked past her and out the door. She swung around to thank the elder, but he was gone. Her hands found her hips as her foot tapped the marble. His appearances and disappearances were becoming a regular occurrence.

The light breeze from outside drifted into the narthex, carrying a faint aroma of roses and frankincense—familiar ingredients in incense. But none was burning in the church. She frowned. Everything seemed to be a mystery around this church.

She stepped outside, the bright sun nearly blinding her. She put on her sunglasses and scanned the busy streets. As expected, Father Apostolos was nowhere to be found.

A knot of people came out of the hotel's door across from her. What if Justin went searching for her? She wasn't sure where to go but spotted Becky heading toward their hotel. She exhaled in relief and jogged over to her.

"Already got your routine church visit in for the day?" Becky asked with a grin.

She took hold of Becky's arm and guided her into their hotel.

Becky raised the arm Christina was holding. "What's with the woman-handling, bestie?"

"I need to talk to you, but we can't stay here for long." Christina surveyed the lobby. "Maybe we should go to one of the local restaurants for a late breakfast."

Becky turned quickly, and Christina released her arm. "That'll work. I haven't eaten yet."

They walked to the nearest open restaurant and found a table for two on the back patio, close to the balcony ledge. The blue awning over the tables protected them from the already hot sun's rays. Christina gazed at the sea where a craft looking like an old pirate ship with its tan sails and wooden body floated along the waves. A few speed boats zipped across the water, sparkling in the white beams of the sun.

Every place on the island had a spectacular view. But Justin's presence tainted it. Anger rose like pulsating heat waves through her. *Go away, Justin.*

A waitress showed up and took their orders of eggs, bread with marmalade, slices of ham, strawberries, yogurt with honey, and *portokaladas* to drink.

"Don't leave me hanging, Christina. What was so urgent you had to throttle me on the street?" Becky scowled, then winked.

Christina picked up her napkin and folded it into strange shapes.

Becky watched her. "Uh-oh. Must be a doozy."

"I should've told you last night, but I was drained and didn't wait up for you."

Becky leaned her forearms on the table and raised a hand. "Well?"

"Justin showed up at our hotel room last night."

Becky's jaw dropped. "Say what?"

"Yeah."

"Why in the whole universe is he here?"

"Supposedly to make up."

One of Becky's brows rose. "You're kidding, right?"

"No. He didn't sound like he was kidding. He sounded pitiful, actually." Christina shook out her napkin and laid it flat on the table, smoothing it down over and over again. "In fact, he looked pretty crappy."

"Good. He should look and feel crappy after what he did to you."

"I think he did."

"Did you tell him to get lost? Jump in the Aegean and swim for Athens?"

"Not quite, but I did tell him to leave our room."

"It's better than nothing."

"He left me alone but said he'd call me around eleven today so we could meet and talk some more." Christina ground her teeth. "Like I would want to discuss anything with him."

Becky glanced at her watch. "It's nearly noon. Have you checked your phone?"

Christina pulled out her cell from her purse, and three text messages appeared on the screen. "He's been trying to reach me since ten forty-five."

Becky sighed. "Well, you can't hide from him forever. It's a small island. He knows where you're staying."

Christina cringed. "And he's hunted me down all the way over here."

The waitress arrived with their meals, and they ate in silence for a few minutes.

Becky bit into a strawberry and looked skyward, as if in thought. "Yeah. That's quite a haul he's made. Must be really desperate to see you." She paused and looked at Christina with a sober expression. "How'd he know you were here?"

"Talked my dad into telling him. Sweetened him up with words of making things right."

"Oh yeah. Your dad was pretty ticked over the divorce. But you never told him about Justin's cheating. That would've changed his mind."

"It wasn't something I wanted to share." Frowning, Christina wiped her mouth with the cloth napkin. "It's embarrassing being cheated on. Like there's something wrong with me even though I know that's not true. It's just embedded in me or something."

"It's embedded in a lot of women, and it shouldn't be."

Becky tapped her fingers on the table and raised her brows. "What's your plan for this clown?"

Christina shrugged. "I don't know. I already told him it's too late. But it was like I hadn't said it."

"More likely, he wasn't listening. Never was good at that."

"You're right."

"Well, he's in your past, part of the unimpressive relics of your romantic history. Keep his dusty old self in those ancient storage shelves. Better yet, sweep the crumbling remains out the rickety door and padlock the sucker."

Christina sighed, leaning an elbow on the table and palm against her forehead. "I just want him to go away. Leave the island."

"Of course you do. Who wouldn't?"

"He's ruining my vacation."

"Why don't you tell him what you told me?"

"I'll try. I've got to work up the courage and stomach to meet with him. It'll be somewhere public, not back in my hotel room. Never again."

"Good move. Nice hotel rooms aren't for snakes."

"This island isn't the place for snakes."

Becky let out a booming laugh. "Even better."

They finished brunch and headed to their hotel room. Christina opened the door and entered with Becky behind her. She spotted her sketchbook still lying on the table on the balcony. Thank God it hadn't been rained on or blown away, although rain was sparse in the summer on Santorini.

She brought the notebook and pencil inside. The items reminded her of Nathan. She hugged the sketchpad against her chest.

"Been drawing again?" Becky asked, flopping on the bed, leaning against the pillows and headboard.

"I went to the outlook yesterday afternoon and saw Nathan there painting." Her mouth curved upward. "I didn't know he painted."

"How could you have? You'd barely given him the chance to say hello to you at lunch the other day, let alone ask about his hobbies."

Christina waved a dismissive hand at Becky and set the sketchpad and pencil on the desk. "That changed yesterday."

Becky sat up. "Oh?"

"We had a nice talk about art. Painting, drawing. Our love of them. He was so sweet, and his painting of the caldera was incredible."

A slow, sneaky smile slid across Becky's face. "So, he wasn't so bad after all, huh?"

Christina's face warmed. Nathan's face close to hers filled her head, and the scrumptious scent of him revisited her senses, causing her body to float as if on air. *Not bad at all.* She grinned and shook her head.

"You going to get together with him soon?"

"I think I'd like to." *Think?* Who was she kidding? There was no doubt she wouldn't mind another one of those intimate encounters with him. She nodded and waved a hand at Becky. "After all, I was told to follow your advice."

"And so you did." Becky clapped her hands together. "Nice work, girl."

Christina reached for the notebook. "I sketched him when he was busy with his painting." She giggled. "Let me show you." She flipped through the pages to the picture of the horizon, then looped it over the spiral holding the papers together. The next page was blank, but tiny scraps of her picture of Nathan were still tucked in the metal spring. She caught her breath.

Becky left the bed and stood next to her. "What? What is it?"

"It's gone." Christina fingered the paper remnants of where the sheet had been torn out. Her stomach knotted. "It was here last night."

Becky turned toward the balcony. "Somebody climbed on our balcony and took your drawing? Who would've done such an asinine thing?"

Justin had visited her before she'd gone to bed for the night. He knew what room she was in. He probably didn't like the reception he'd gotten from her. "Bet it was Justin."

Becky snapped her fingers, then pointed at Christina. "Best

guess ever." She put her hands on her hips. "Probably saw the picture of gorgeous Nathan and went berserk."

"He was always pretty possessive and the biggest hypocrite alive."

"Hundred percent right, the cheater." Becky scowled.

Christina set the notebook on the desk and dropped into the chair. "What should I do?"

"Set up a meeting place and time and call out his ass."

"Can we go to the beach first? I need some sunshine before the storm."

"You better believe it." Becky headed to the bathroom. "Let's get ready."

"I'm right behind you." Christina gathered her suntan lotion and towel, placing them in her large, empty art bag. She pulled out her bathing suit from the top drawer in the wardrobe and mulled over how she'd approach Justin after her respite of lounging in the sun and listening to the rolling waves hit the shore.

Chapter Fifteen

Nathan walked down the wide, white steps descending toward Amoudi Bay, with George by his side.

"Only two hundred and ninety-seven of these to go," George said with a snicker.

Nathan rolled his eyes.

George lifted one of his thick legs. "It's good for the legs, man."

"No doubt."

"We just hiked all over Fira. I think we can handle going down some stairs."

"I'm keeping my focus on that little restaurant." Nathan pointed toward it, below them, to the left. "I need to refuel."

They continued down the steps and stopped at the bottom, moving to the side for a couple of people on donkeys.

Nathan tented his eyes with his hand, squinting at the animals and their human cargo. "Why didn't we rent one of those?"

George clapped a hand on his shoulder. "Really?" He guffawed. "Do they look more comfortable than using our own feet?"

Nathan shrugged. "Would've been something different."

George cocked his head to the side and folded his arms. "This, coming from a creature of habit. You and spontaneity don't know each other."

"I can be spontaneous."

George chuckled. "That would be a first."

"Let's just get something to eat before I spontaneously leave you here alone." Nathan smirked, then strode toward the restaurant.

"Hey, I'm all in for grub."

Near the pier, Nathan spotted Christina and her friend. After what happened yesterday, having to abruptly leave their conversation, he felt compelled to apologize to her. The small waves of the sea slapped against the sides of the cement harbor. He'd have to risk being that near the water to talk to her. His muscles tightened, and he rolled his shoulders. *Get a grip and go say sorry.* "Hold on. I need to talk to Christina."

"What?" George whipped his head from side to side. "Where is she? Is Becky with her?"

Nathan pointed toward the women. "They're over there."

George bent his knees and bounced like a spring, the heels of his sneakers thumping the ground. "What are we waiting for?" he asked with a goofy grin. "Let's go." He sauntered forward with a clumsy gait.

Nathan caught up with him and approached Christina. She and Becky were facing the Aegean, their backs to him and George.

Christina's long, yellow sundress rippled in the light breeze. The top portion of her raven hair was pinned back with a large barrette while the rest of her hair danced from side to side. The delicious, alluring aroma of tangerines and flowers mixed with suntan lotion emanating from her teased his nostrils.

George put an arm around Becky and turned her to face him. She shrieked and wrapped her arms around his bulky torso.

Nathan tapped Christina's shoulder. She swung around with a look of confusion, but once her eyes locked with his, the perplexed expression fell away, her eyes softened, her lips parted just a little, and her face brightened. His body transformed into the consistency of applesauce, and he couldn't help but smile. Such a switch in her response from a couple of days ago. But he'd realized he had changed also. He'd become as pliable as wet clay around her ever since she'd shown up at the precipice and actually sat with him, sharing her love of art. He could hardly believe it had happened, but looking into her eyes now, he knew it had. His heart ballooned with intensity, electricity streaking through him.

She gave him a sexy smile, her taupe lips smooth and lush, kissable, more than ever before, but he woke himself from whatever spell she had over him and straightened his stance, making sure he focused on why he'd approached her.

"Hey, Christina. I'm sorry I had to cut our talk short yesterday. Can't believe I forgot I had lunch plans."

She swept hair off her shoulder. "It's okay. We're both here on vacation with our own schedules." She looked away, her cheeks glowing light pink. "I just hope we can pick up where we left off with the art."

Her words were so soft he'd nearly not heard her. She wanted to spend more time with him. He grinned.

"Nate, I invited Becky to eat lunch with us. How about Christina?"

George's voice came out of nowhere, puncturing the delirious bubble he'd been in. What was wrong with him? He was acting like a teenager. Had he not learned from his past girlfriends who had all been attractive? Lured him right in, then tossed him in the trash when things didn't go their way. He glanced at Christina while her attention was on Becky and George. How would she be any different than those other women?

"Christina, you want to join them?" Becky's features took on a look of concern, her brow furrowed and hand on her friend's shoulder. "I know you had something you needed to do."

Christina's friendly smile and gentle gaze disappeared, and something akin to fear and irritation lit those dark eyes.

Damn. He hadn't even thought about what plans she had for

the day. George didn't bother to ask either. He glared at his impulsive friend.

"I'm sorry. We didn't know you already had plans," he said.

Christina shook her head and waved a hand. "Oh no. It's fine." She flicked a look at her friend.

Nathan frowned. What was going on with this woman?

"We already ate a little while ago—"

"I'll pick up something to go if you want to take a walk with me," Nathan said, urgency thudding in his chest. He didn't want to lose this opportunity. God, he was an idiot.

Her beautiful smile returned, sending his spirits soaring.

"Okay."

"What do you want to do, George?" Becky asked.

"Eat." He chuckled.

Becky put her hand in his, and before turning to head toward the restaurant, she glanced back at Christina. "We'll meet back at the hotel in a few hours, if that works for you."

"It does."

Becky pointed a finger at Christina. "Just don't forget to get that… that thing done."

Christina huffed. "I won't."

Nathan titled his head to the side, puzzled, as George and Becky strolled toward the eatery.

Christina's phone vibrated and buzzed loud enough that he could hear it. She jumped, pulling the mobile out of one of her pockets. She stared at the screen, her mouth in a tight line, then pressed a button on the side of the phone and shoved it back in her pocket. "Sorry. I know how annoying and rude phone messages can be in the middle of conversations. I shut it down."

He didn't want to be nosy, so he nodded and gestured toward the restaurant even though her distressed expression from reading the text niggled at him. Why? What was he getting himself into? He had no idea, and it bothered him. Still, he kept his feelings to himself and ordered his food.

NATHAN WALKED WITH CHRISTINA ALONG THE BAY, MAKING SURE HE was as far from the water as he could be without looking strange. Christina didn't seem to notice his aversion, and he liked it that way. George and Becky were still eating at the restaurant. He'd finished his gyro and fries a few minutes earlier and dropped the trash into the nearest receptacle.

"Have you done any other paintings since yesterday?" Christina asked.

"No. I haven't had time. But I'll make some." Nathan slid his hands in his pockets while they walked toward the three hundred white steps. "There are plenty of days left on the island for painting more."

"I'm planning to draw several pictures of the churches and lovely flowers around here. There are so many."

Nathan nodded.

Christina's brows knitted as if she were confused or in deep thought. She then looked at him with those profound, ebony eyes. "Was that woman you ate lunch with a close friend of yours?"

He paused, his face warming. Her question had caught him off guard. It was a personal question he'd never have expected from her, having been so aloof until yesterday. Something had obviously changed with her. Unsure how he felt about it, caution rolled through his gut.

"I'm sorry." Christina shook her head and waved a hand. "I'm prying."

"No, it's okay." Thalia was, after all, just a friend. "Yes, she's a friend of mine from my childhood. Her name is Thalia."

Christina clasped her hands together between her hips. "Pretty name." Her lips pressed together, and Nathan wondered if she really meant what she'd said.

"I came to Greece many times when I was a child, to visit my papou... er, that's grandfather in Greek."

"Yes, I know."

She knew. An image of her in the church near their hotel came back to him. Maybe she was an Orthodox Christian too.

"My yiayia lives up north, in Kalavryta," she said.

"My papou lives in Athens."

"Does this mean you get to see him before you head back to the States?"

"Yes. That's the plan." He smiled.

Nathan peered at the endless steps. "You up for the climb, or do you want to take a different route?"

"Let's give it a try."

As they ascended the stairs, the blistering sun roasted his back. Today would have been great if the breeze was much stronger. He wiped his forehead and walked alongside Christina, the sound of waves lapping against the pier behind them, along with the shuffling of their shoes on the ivory steps. What would they do when they got to the top? Maybe he could convince her to come with him on a short jaunt through Pyrgos. That was his favorite little village on the island. A painter's dream.

He stopped and clenched his jaw. *You're in fantasy land again.*

"Do you need to rest?" Christina asked, gazing down, two steps above him. A smile played on her beautiful lips. "We've only gone up ten so far."

He laughed, working to hide his frustration. "Rest? Are you kidding?" He moved up to the step where she stood. "Let's get to at least a hundred before you ask me that question."

Christina grinned. "It's a deal."

He breathed in the fragrance of her as they continued up the wide blocks.

A COUPLE OF STEPS OVER A HUNDRED, CHRISTINA LEANED AGAINST one of the sides of the ascending walkway and blew out a breath. She plucked a tissue from her purse and mopped her perspiring forehead and neck. Two more people on donkeys clopped by them on their way up the never-ending steps.

"Maybe we should've taken those," she said.

"You chose to walk, remember?" He grinned, those dimples teasing her.

"So I made a mistake." She glanced up, shielding her eyes from the sweltering sun. "I didn't realize how hot it was going to be today."

"We can go back down and take a cab up, if you'd like. It beats riding donkeys."

The nearly two hundred more steps loomed ahead of them, and Nathan's suggestion sounded better by the minute. "Let's do that." She pivoted on her heel and began the descent to the bottom.

Nathan marched down next to her with some urgency. He must have been just as desperate to get back to level ground as she was. They ran down the last several steps, as if racing each other to the finish line.

Giggles erupted from her throat, and she raised her arms above her head. "I won!"

Nathan put a hand on his hip, leaning his weight on his right leg and tilting his head to the side. Sweat glistened on his face and neck. He panted a bit but smiled. "No, you didn't. We tied."

She laughed, leaning over, catching her breath, her hands on her knees. "Sure we did." She pointed at the last step. "You saw me jump over the last step and land here before you even got to it."

He ran an arm over his forehead. "Okay, okay. But it was close."

"I'll give you that."

George and Becky approached them.

"What have you guys been doing? You're drenched," Becky said.

"We were going to walk up all those stairs, but it got to be too much in this heat," Christina said.

"I bet. Climbing ten of those huge honkers would've done me in." Becky cocked her head toward a taxi rolling toward them. "Hop in with us. We're going to the top."

"Great." Christina climbed in the back seat of the cab, in between Nathan and Becky. George sat in the front.

When they arrived at their hotel, George draped an arm around Becky's small shoulders. "We're gonna change, then check out some of the stores."

"Okay." Nathan looked down at her with those gorgeous eyes. "Would you like to take a short trip to Pyrgos with me? Walk through those little winding passageways?"

Christina's heart swelled as she gazed up at him. How she'd changed her view of him the past twenty-four hours was beyond her. Then she remembered Becky's words about letting go. She'd actually done it.

"I'd love—"

"Christina." The familiar, nauseating voice of her ex-husband came from behind her. She tensed, squeezing her eyes shut. *Why won't he just go away?* He meant nothing to her. His showing up now told her it was a sign for her to tell him so.

She swung around. "Give me a minute."

Justin scratched his head with a scowl on his face.

"Looks like you've already got plans." Nathan stared at Justin as if he were a pesky insect.

Could he be jealous? A part of her, admittedly, tingled over that possibility. She shook herself out of it. It was fine to let go, but not to the point of losing her senses.

"Yes. I'll have to take a rain check on your offer."

"That's fine. I'll see you around." Nathan nodded his head, jaw twitching. He slid his hands in his pockets and strolled down the sidewalk toward the stores.

Justin moved in front of her view of Nathan's retreating figure. "Why didn't you answer my texts?" He jerked a nod back toward Nathan. "Too busy with him?"

Anger streaked through every part of her. "Yeah, I was." She folded her arms across her chest. "Remember, we're divorced. You left me for another woman."

The muscles in his neck tightened like thin cable cords, and he raised his chin in defiance.

She bobbed her head side to side, her focus on the area behind him. "By the way, where is she?"

His features softened with a wounded look in his eyes. "She's not here." He lowered his gaze. "I made a mistake divorcing you for her."

Christina tapped her foot, her arms still tightly crossed. "You think?"

He moved closer to her, leaving only a foot of space between them. Christina avoided his stare, turning her head slightly to the left, watching the tourists spill out of some stores and disappear into others.

"Come on. Can't we go someplace and talk?"

An upsetting scene from her past played through her head. In their old house, Justin loomed near the bed, where she lay in a tight ball, tears streaming down her face. An aching wave of familiar grief pressed against her chest.

He'd curled his lip in disgust. "You should be over this by now. I'm not going to keep coming home to this every day." Eyes glowing with contempt, he'd stomped out of the room and slammed the bedroom door.

He'd been a heartless bastard to her. And now he'd flown here to make a pitiful attempt at a reunion. Another wave of anger radiated through her.

Before she could answer, he reached a hand to touch her chin. She stepped back.

His features hardened, and he glanced over his shoulder. "It's that guy, isn't it?"

Nathan. His image she'd drawn in her sketchpad came back to her. The picture that had been ripped out of her drawing book. She clenched her teeth and fisted her hands. "As a matter of fact, it is." She straightened her back. "You want to talk? Let's talk."

She strode toward one of a café's small patio tables with umbrellas and chairs.

Justin followed and sat across from her.

She raised her chin and folded her forearms on the table.

His brows furrowed, and he licked his lips. "I want to start over, Christina. Give it another shot."

The laugh came out of her without a thought.

"Don't laugh. You're making me feel like an ass."

She laughed again.

He pounded his fist on the table. "Look. I'm trying to have a serious talk with you. Show you I still care and that I've changed." He flattened out his hand on the table, then reached for hers.

She kept her arms crossed; hands tucked out of sight.

He gave her a pleading look. "Couldn't you tell when I showed up last night after traveling thousands of miles to be here with you?"

The bouts of his short temper spitting like fire from him hadn't changed.

"Really? So far, what I've seen is you're the same Justin I divorced nine months ago."

He huffed, his hand balling into a fist again. "I'm not, damn it."

She'd find out how much he changed with her next question. "Did you creep onto my balcony last night and rip out a drawing from my notebook?"

He scowled. "What the hell? Where'd this come from? And why would I care about your drawings?" This time he laughed.

She stiffened and narrowed her eyes at him. "This is how you show me you've changed?"

He sighed loudly. "Can we get back to us instead of your obsessive doodling? It always sucked up all your time. Made me feel like I didn't exist."

She tightened her mouth and tapped her fingers on the table. *Doodling?* "You're not convincing me you didn't take my drawing or that you're no longer an asshole."

He threw his hands up. "This is dumb. I know you've always had trouble keeping focused on stuff, but come on."

She clasped her hands so tightly together they ached. "Keep going. You're doing an excellent job reminding me why we're divorced."

His face fell, and a flicker of realization flashed in his eyes. He looked away and rubbed the back of his neck. "I didn't mean what I said. I was angry."

"That's the problem." She'd had her fill of Justin. She rose from her chair and pushed it back. "You're always angry and verbally abusive." It was time to leave. Their conversation had steered toward the same unhealthy path. Her therapist had worked with her for months, learning to not get sucked into his abusive patterns.

He scrambled out of his seat. "Wait. I'm not done telling you how I feel."

"You're done, Justin. You were done for me a year and a half ago."

She marched off in the direction Nathan had gone, her hands fisted and eyes focused on one of the stores to duck into. She reached a clothing shop and slipped through the narrow opening to the entrance, between knots of people.

She peeked through the window. Justin hadn't followed her. Good. But when would he leave? He was ruining her vacation, and she'd put a stop to it one way or another. She pulled out her phone and texted Becky.

Which beach did you go to?

Perissa. You coming?

No. Where's Nathan? Ask George please.

Okay.

She waited, rocking back and forth, from one foot to the other.

Her phone lit up and binged.

Nathan's at his uncle's shop.

Where's that, and what's the name of the shop?

A block north of Athena Delights restaurant. The store's name is Sea Treasures.

Okay. Thanks.

Christina left the shop, then stopped on the sidewalk. She studied her sundress that covered her bathing suit. Her skin was sticky from being in the hot sun and climbing the large steps earlier. She'd return to the hotel for a quick cleanup and change, then go see Nathan.

Chapter Sixteen

Nathan ran the roller up and down one of the walls in his uncle's office. The striking teal color stood out against the three adjacent white walls yet to be painted.

His uncle appeared at the archway. "When you done with that wall, my boy, close up paint." He pointed at him with a grin. "You working overtime, not regular hours."

"Sure, *Thío*."

"Be back in little bit to see the finished work."

Nathan dipped the roller in the tin pan holding the paint. After collecting enough of the hue, he coated the next section of the wall.

Settling back into the rhythm of his work, his mind wandered to Christina. Who was that guy who'd shown up out of nowhere? He sure seemed like he knew her well… *too well*. Nathan wrinkled his nose, then pushed away the disturbing thoughts and concentrated on the wall. Again, it wasn't his business. If she decided to tell him the next time she saw him, so be it. He wouldn't push.

His heart tightened as he remembered her expression at the sound of that guy's voice. Genuine fear and something akin to sorrow had shone in her dark eyes. And he hadn't missed her face turn pale. Nathan stiffened. He was worrying over her, and she wasn't even his. He bent and pressed more paint onto his roller. He raised his brows and tilted his head to the side. And he didn't belong to her. He needed to let it go, but his heart wouldn't allow him. Gritting his teeth, he swept the remaining wall with wide swaths of the teal paint.

"Nathan, my boy, a young lady here to see you," his uncle called from behind him.

He swung around. Christina stood there in all her beauty, with hands clasped between her curvy hips. A small smile brightened her face.

Just the sight of her made his heart skip a beat. Reflexively he pressed his hand against his chest. Where had that guy gone? Did it matter now that she was there?

"Christina. Hey." He set down the roller in the pan and walked over to her. "How'd you find me?"

"Texted Becky, and she asked George."

"Oh right. I'd let him know I'd come here after I left you and… uh… the man you were talking to."

Her lips pursed together. "Are you still offering that short jaunt to Pyrgos?"

She didn't want to talk about the guy. His worries about the mystery man fell away, and excitement coursed through him. "Yes. Definitely, yes."

"Well." She spread out her arms, looking down at her soft, pink blouse, tan shorts, and back at him. "I'm ready to go when you are."

Nathan pictured her in his arms. He was more than ready to go with her, but the painting supplies on the floor glared at him. He couldn't leave without cleaning up first. "I'm sorry, but could you give me about fifteen minutes? I need to finish up here and talk to my uncle."

"Sure. Meet me in the hotel's lobby?"

He grinned. "That would be perfect."

"All right. See you soon." She bit her lip, then hurried out of the room.

"Yep."

She seemed nervous. Had that guy caused it? He swatted at the air. Nevertheless, things had certainly changed in a matter of a half hour. He didn't fight the smile spreading across his face as he picked up the pan and roller and took it to the sink in the bathroom.

CHRISTINA STROLLED DOWN THE SIDEWALK, PASSING A STREAM OF people. The aroma of souvlaki wafted out of a restaurant on her right. She took in the delicious smell while wiping her damp forehead from the unrelenting sun threatening to bake her. She sat on a bench outside the restaurant and pulled out suntan lotion from her large purse.

Rubbing a generous amount on her arm, she watched the crowded sidewalks, the chatter and laughter of the people muffled by a couple of mopeds rumbling by. She wanted to get lost in the scene—forget that her ex-husband was still on the island. Applying lotion on her other arm, she huffed. He should already be taking a ferry back to Athens. Christina raised her brows. Maybe he was packing and getting ready to leave for the port. After all, she'd left no doubts that they were finished and done with ages ago. She put the sun block back in her purse, got up, and resumed walking toward her hotel.

Uneasiness pressed on her chest as a chill ran through her. Was someone following her? Her muscles tensed, and a sinking feeling settled in the pit of her stomach. She spared a quick glance over her shoulder. Only strangers surrounded her, going into the restaurant she left, while others gathered in knots on the pavement. She faced the street ahead of her and focused on her hotel a block away. The feeling of being watched and followed came back like a thick, menacing wave of heat. This time she didn't look back.

It had been wishful thinking Justin would get the message. But he wasn't going to win. She straightened her posture.

Christina's strides grew faster as she reached the hotel's double doors, and she pushed one of them open. She slipped through and marched into the lobby, turning to face the doors. In the minute she stood there, no one entered the hotel. She hurried to the stairs, climbed them two at a time, then rushed to her hotel room.

If Justin came knocking at the door, she'd ignore it, pretend she wasn't there.

Christina checked her watch. Nathan would be in the lobby in less than ten minutes. She'd leave her room soon. Relief washed over her, thankful Nathan was taking her to Pyrgos. Nathan. The strange man she'd thought might have been stalking her just a few short days ago. She laughed under her breath. My, how things had changed in such a short period of time.

No rapping came at her door in the next few minutes. Exhaling, she left her room and headed to the lobby.

SHE REACHED THE LOBBY AND SPOTTED NATHAN SITTING IN ONE OF the contemporary leather chairs in the open space. He stood when she approached him.

His cobalt-blue eyes sparkled, and he gave her a wobbly-leg-inducing smile, scrumptious dimples and all. "You ready?"

She pressed a hand to her chest, her heart thudding against it. *Crap.* What was wrong with her? Becky's words, *let yourself go,* came back to her. It was her friend's fault she'd weakened her defenses.

"Christina?" Nathan tilted his head to the side, gazing at her expectantly.

Warmth filled her. An invisible force tugged at her—she was completely drawn to him. Was this a sign?

He touched her arm, and it tingled, sending sparks throughout her body. She stepped back, light-headed.

"Hey, are you okay?" A crease settled between his dark brows.

She needed to get ahold of herself. They were simply going for a walk through a small village. And Justin wouldn't know where she was. That helped clear the confusion. "Yes. Sorry. Let's go."

He gestured toward the door, and she moved ahead of him. He followed her outside, back into the heat of the late-afternoon sun.

Pulling out his phone, he tapped his screen. "Do you want to take a cab or a moped?"

"Cab is fine."

THEY REACHED THE MAIN STREET OF PYRGOS TEN MINUTES LATER, exited the cab, then set out toward one of the ascending ivory paths.

Nathan motioned her with a sweep of his hand to walk ahead of him through the first covered passageway on the sidewalk. Giving him a smile of appreciation, she moved past him.

A small shop angled to the left of the path held porcelain and glass objects.

"Oh, I'd like to go in there," Christina said, clasping her hands together.

"You got it." Nathan opened the door for her, and she entered the store.

She went straight for the mini churches made of porcelain. "My mom gave me one like these she'd gotten from a Greek festival back home."

He nodded. "The top comes off to put a tea candle in, right?"

"Yes." Christina ran her fingers over the blue-domed roof and down the white, rounded side of the chapel. Images of her talk with the abbess came back to her. It seemed like something that had taken place ages ago. Her heart sank. What had happened to that burning calling she'd experienced when she was younger and there earlier on the island? Christina frowned. Was this another sign?

Confusion muddled her brain, and she squeezed her eyes shut, pushing the thoughts aside. She willed herself to live in the moment, let go of overthinking things.

Nathan pointed at the church. "Do you want it?"

She shook her head. "Oh no. I don't need another one. I was just admiring its beauty."

"It is that." Nathan brushed a thumb across his stubbled chin. "I can get it for you if you change your mind."

"That's very kind of you, but I'm going to look around at some other things."

"Okay."

She moved to the decorative plates with paintings of Santorini on them while he thumbed through a book on Greek sculptures a couple of feet away.

The bas relief of a blue-domed church with a huge cross on the top and the cerulean sea and orange sun in the background fanned across the plate caught Christina's interest. She picked it up, along with its holder. "I've got what I want."

Nathan looked up from the glossy book and nodded with a grin.

They headed to the cashier, he graciously paid, and they stepped back onto the narrow white slate path.

Christina sensed Nathan was taking in every part of her backside as they ascended the inclined walk that curved toward the top of a flat roof. Her sandals didn't have good grip, so she groped for the side of the building on her right.

"Let me help."

Nathan held out his hand, and she took it. Tingling ran through her body again as he led her up the path to the cement roof.

Once on the level ground, Christina gazed at the island's rocky and hilly landscape below, meeting the sea at the bottom. The setting sun's rays transformed all of it into a rosy tint. The breeze had picked up, sweeping her hair from the sides of her face, the fresh air brushing across her. She closed her eyes and inhaled the scent of flowers and the salty sea. She hadn't let go of Nathan's hand. It was too comforting not to keep holding on. He made her forget all her worries, all the stressors over future plans.

Her eyes opened, and she captured a glimpse of him.

Nathan looked straight ahead. His handsome profile, with his long, dark lashes, sculpted jaw, and tanned cheek were lit up from the sun. His sable hair fluttered from the wind. She ached to run her hands through his thick locks.

He turned to face her, his sparkling blue eyes meeting her dark ones. All their surroundings melted away as she lost herself in his intense gaze, glowing with what looked like desire. He moved closer, closing his eyes. She shut hers as his lips touched hers, soft and gentle.

Nathan ended the kiss, pulling back slowly.

She opened her eyes halfway, studying his beautiful face. With quivering legs, her heart beating faster than a derby horse's hooves, she wrapped her arms around his neck and pressed her lips to his once more. His fingers grasped her hips before he gathered her in his arms and fully captured her mouth. She surrendered effortlessly to him, their tongues meeting in a tantalizing dance. Warmth spread through her floating body.

When they released each other, Christina swayed, drunk with euphoria. Never had anyone kissed her like that. She sighed and gazed at him. His sensual lips were parted, and his eyes gave off a dark glint of ardor.

"Christina, you're beautiful," he said in a breathless voice.

With muscles morphed into flowing milk, she could barely raise her hand to his stubbly cheek. "So are you." It was a stupid thing to say, but her mind wasn't working. Only her heart was able to respond.

He folded her in his arms again for an all-encompassing embrace. She held him tightly, her cheek against his whiskered one. His heart pattered against hers, their chests nearly meshing into one.

What was happening between them? Whatever it was left her in a marshmallow state.

She peered out at the horizon, the sun half swallowed up by the sea, its orange and pink rays splaying across the sky like an abstract painting.

This had to mean something. Something significant. Her path had definitely changed.

They released each other, and Nathan took her hand in his again, leading her back down the trail.

Back at Pyrgos's main thoroughfare, groups of vacationers gathered at outdoor restaurants and came out of small, colorful shops. Christina and Nathan headed to one of them near a parking lot where a dozen mopeds were lined up against a metal railing.

Nathan looked down at her with twinkling eyes. "Want to go for a spin around the island?"

She shoved her shopping bag into her large purse, then hugged his arm, lacing her fingers with his. "Yes."

"It would cool us off," he said with a chuckle.

"Not only from the sun." She gave him a playful smile, her heart fluttering.

Nathan flashed a gorgeous grin.

He paid the owner of the bike shop, then pulled out one of the blue mopeds. He got on and patted the seat behind him. She straddled the bike, pressing her thighs into his and wrapping her arms around his waist. With her chest against his strong back, a river of fire streaked through her, settling in her belly.

The bike came to life, and he steered them down the quaint streets out of Pyrgos and onto Thira.

The refreshing breeze caressed her face, the rumbling of the bike under her, lulling her into complete relaxation while the pink sky bathed her with its gentle warmth. She couldn't imagine feeling anything better, being anywhere better than where she was at that moment.

They continued through the busy streets of Thira and onto the equally crowded streets of Oia, passing the church she visited so often, their hotel, the Athena Delights restaurant, Nathan's uncle's store, and looped around past a few more churches, homes, shops, and small fields of wildflowers, the scent of them sweetening the air.

When they'd returned the bike and took a cab back to their hotel, their hands intertwined again as they walked into the lobby. They entered the elevator, and Nathan pressed the second-floor button.

Alone in the intimate space, she hugged him. "Thanks for an incredible afternoon, Nathan."

"You're welcome. It was the best day I've had in a long time."

"Me too," she whispered in his ear.

The doors opened.

He squeezed her, then let her go. "See you tomorrow?"

"Yes. We could meet at the lookout for some artistic collaboration." She smiled, filled with so much joy her jaw began to ache.

"What time? Ten? Eleven?"

"Eleven would be good."

"Great." He leaned down and gave her a gentle kiss. "See you then."

She nodded, placing a hand on her cheek, as she watched him head down the hall to his room. Yes, her plans had taken a drastic, delicious change. She could barely wait to see where this new path led her.

Chapter Seventeen

N athan lay in bed that night, his body loose and relaxed.
Images of Christina filled his head from their outing
together. Her ebony doe eyes, beautiful smile, and shiny raven
hair sent electric currents through him. He could still feel her arms
around him on the moped, her cheek against his, their intense kiss
that sent his heart thudding, his body aching in response. He
rolled onto his side. It had all been so good, like a fantasy, unreal.
Would it turn out to be just that? Not real? Would Christina be
like Jennifer and the others?

He turned on his back and scowled. No. She wasn't like
Jennifer. And he wouldn't be lured in and manipulated again. He
wasn't that same, naive guy. He'd keep his wits about him. But
he'd have to admit that after holding Christina in his arms,
kissing her, talking with her, it would be a huge challenge. Nathan
inhaled, then blew out a cleansing breath. He was up to it.

In the morning, Nathan collected his art paraphernalia and
put them in his duffel bag. A knock came at his door. He opened it
and found Thalia there.

She gave him a wide grin and waved. "Are you ready for beach and shells?"

Crap. He'd forgotten he'd told Thalia he'd have time on Saturday for her. Guilt ate at him as she stared expectantly, her body swaying back and forth.

Glancing at the bag of art supplies and sighing, he had to do what was right. He'd promised Thalia before making plans with Christina. But he'd need to tell Christina.

He held up a finger. "Can you give me a minute?"

"Okay." Her tone reflected skepticism.

"I just need to let Christina know."

"Why?"

"I accidentally made plans with her."

Thalia raised her brows.

"I have to let her know we need to change our plans. Be right back." He pointed at his door. "Would you wait there?"

She shrugged but leaned against the wall next to the door.

Okay, so she wasn't thrilled about his lapse in memory, but her response wasn't altogether negative.

He jogged down the hall to the room number George had told him was Christina and Becky's. He rapped on the door with urgency.

The door opened slowly, as if the women were hesitant to let anyone in.

Christina peeked her head out of the six-inch-wide crack. Her face lit up, and she pulled the door wider. "Hi. You're early."

His stomach twisted. She looked so happy. "I'm sorry. I forgot I'd made plans with my friend Thalia."

The cheerfulness and light left her eyes, and her mouth turned slightly down. "Oh."

"Nathan, you coming?" Thalia called from his door.

Christina's gaze lowered. "Have fun." Her face disappeared from the opening, and the door began to close.

Nathan put a hand on the door and slid into her room.

Christina let go, and it clunked shut. The shower was going, and he assumed Becky was in the bathroom.

Christina combed a hand through her long hair, glancing up at him. "It's okay, Nathan. I understand."

He put his hands on her arms. "We can meet up this afternoon for our art collaboration."

A smile lit her face, her eyes shining. "Great. What time?"

"How about two?"

"Meet you at the lookout?"

"You got it."

"Nathan," Thalia called again.

He slipped out the door, held up a hand, and cast a quick look at his friend. "Coming." His gaze returned to Christina. He leaned in and whispered in her ear, "I'll see you in a few hours."

She giggled. "All right."

Truth be told, if Becky weren't still there, he'd rather have stayed with Christina in her room and gotten to know her even more intimately. But his dreams didn't make his reality. He hurried toward Thalia, and they headed to the lobby.

NATHAN WALKED WITH THALIA ALONG THE BEACH, PICKING UP shells and pebbles. It brought back memories of his childhood, and he smiled. That old, familiar feeling of close friendship warmed his soul. Thalia had been like one of the boys then. A buddy who played tag, climbed the playground equipment, and raced him to the ice cream vendors on the street corners. She'd been a loyal, good friend, and here she was, carrying on where they'd left off years ago.

"Look at this one. It beautiful," Thalia said, holding up a large half seashell.

"That's a good one." He rolled a medium-sized pebble in his hand and stood a good distance from the shore. Stifling the uneasiness in his belly over being close to the water, he launched the stone toward it. A wave swallowed the pebble.

She laughed. "Poor rock."

He chuckled. "There are a lot more where that came from." He grabbed another one off the sandy, rocky shore.

Nathan curved his arm and threw the pebble toward the sea. It sliced through a small wave, then sank under the water. "Ha." He grinned.

Thalia snorted. "Okay. Your rock beat first wave this time."

"Yep."

Her brows lifted. "You and Christina getting close, eh?"

Thalia's question had come out of nowhere. All the same, he beamed just from the sound of Christina's name. Boy, he was falling hard for this woman.

"You're smiling. So, yes?" Thalia flashed a teasing grin.

Nathan picked up another pebble and sent it sailing across the rolling sea, sinking seconds later. His body tingled, remembering Christina's soft lips against his. He'd say that was pretty close. "We're getting to know each other. And yeah, it's been… great." His face heated.

Thalia squatted and plucked up another shell. Standing, she ran her fingers over the grooves in the rounded shard. She raised her head, and her brown eyes met his blue ones. "She is nice then?"

"Yes. Very." He remembered their first real conversation at the restaurant. Christina had been an iceberg. He chuckled under his breath. Yet he didn't know what had caused her about-face. He would have to ask her later when they got together at the precipice.

"She not coming on the boat with us, yes?"

The boat tour. Nathan had nearly forgotten about that. His stomach knotted at the thought. The last time he'd pondered the boat excursion, he'd planned to use Thalia as a buffer between him and Christina. He laughed softly again. He definitely wouldn't need a buffer now. Dark images of the craft rocking on the Aegean made him queasy. He pushed the thoughts away and picked up a cylindrical, swirly seashell.

"Yes, she is, along with her friend Becky. George invited them."

"Oh." She lowered her gaze as her foot tapped a stone embedded in the sand.

Nathan dusted off the sand stuck to the shell. "George can never be around too many women."

Thalia snickered.

He sat on the rocky ground. Thalia joined him.

"Beautiful, yes?" she said, staring at the sea.

"Yes." But his gaze didn't linger on the water. He rubbed the shell with his thumb, his mind already on the anticipated meeting with Christina at the lookout.

"I'm so glad you ask me to come on the boat with you." She laid a hand on his shoulder and squeezed it. "It will be something special I will remember of our time together here."

Nathan patted her hand on his shoulder and didn't allow thoughts of the boat to enter his mind. "It will be a special memory for me too. It's been so long since we last did anything fun together."

She turned to face him. "Oh, this is so true." Her eyes glistened. "It too bad you live far away."

He dug his heels into the sand. "It does put a damper on hanging out together."

Thalia faced the sea again, drawing up her knees and wrapping her arms around them. "Yes."

Nathan checked his watch. It was nearly time for him to meet George at the hotel's restaurant for lunch.

"What is it?" Thalia asked.

"I've got to get going. I'm meeting George for lunch."

"Ah." Thalia smiled. "Sure."

He got up and held out a hand for her to grab. She took it, and he helped her stand. They headed toward the path out of the area. Thalia glanced at him and gave his arm an affectionate squeeze. He pointed toward the inclined trail, and she moved ahead of him toward it. In a couple of hours, he'd meet Christina. His steps quickened, along with his heartbeat.

Chapter Eighteen

Christina sat on the balcony, eating a gyro and fries. A bottle of *lemonada* sat next to the dish of food.

She gazed out at the clear azure water, the sun shining in the cloudless sky. The sea breeze was light and comforting, the temperature more bearable than yesterday.

In a couple of hours, she'd meet with Nathan at the lookout. She swayed in her chair, excitement flowing through her body.

Becky came out on the terrace and sat in the chair across from her, setting a plate and bottle on the table.

"Girl, you're chipper, googly-eyed with goofy grins lately." She stuffed a fry in her mouth and gave Christina a look of approval. "See what happens when you follow your bestie's advice?"

"Yes. I become a marshmallow." Christina sniggered.

"A mushy brain isn't bad if you're tied to a hunk like Nathan."

"I don't think I'm tied to him though."

"No. Of course not. Those lopsided grins and thousand-mile stares are indigestion."

Christina couldn't help but laugh. "Okay, okay." Yet her thoughts wandered to what would come of this budding relationship with Nathan. Would it stick? Was it supposed to?

Had she neglected her calling to the monastic life? And there was Justin. Thankful he hadn't bothered her since yesterday afternoon, she hoped he'd stay away today. However, it was too much to expect that he'd already left the island.

"So much for the cheery face," Becky muttered.

"Hmm?"

"You look like you ate a lemon, rind and all."

"It's Justin. I want him to disappear."

"Too bad I'm not a magician."

Christina took a sip of soda. "The fact that he's still on the island dampens my mood."

"Yeah. Probably because he's a pain in the ass."

"I think he got the message, though, that I didn't want anything to do with him."

"So what's the worry, other than his carcass inhabiting the same patch of land as you?"

"I don't know. It just bugs me that he's here."

"Forget about him. He's not worth a second of your thoughts."

Christina left her chair and leaned her elbows on the balcony ledge. "What a mess this vacation has become. So complicated, when vacations are supposed to be the opposite."

Becky came alongside her. "It doesn't have to be complicated. Remember?" She fluttered her fingers. "Let things go."

Christina faced her friend. "There's only so much letting go I can do."

"I know it's hard for you, but see how great it's turned out so far?"

Christina shook her head and looked down at the hydrangea bushes below the balcony. A wadded sheet of paper sat wedged between the flowers. She gasped.

"What? What's it now?" Becky leaned over the ledge and looked down.

Christina reached toward the bush, but her fingers only grazed the paper. She groaned and stared at Becky.

"Don't look at me. You're four inches taller."

"You could help by boosting me up a bit."

"That I can do."

Christina leaned her stomach against the ledge while Becky kept a good grip on her legs. She reached out again, her fingers touching the white ball. Stretching another inch, her hand covered the sheet and plucked it out of the bush.

"Pull me up," she said.

"Aye, aye, captain."

Christina's shoes landed on the solid floor of the balcony. She held up the paper. "Got it."

"Hope it was worth getting."

She opened the paper, spread it on the table, and smoothed out the wrinkles as best she could. The sketch of Nathan with a large red X slicing through his figure stood out through the crinkles.

Her stomach twisted. *Who did this?* Her mouth tightened. Justin of course. He'd acted innocent, but it was like him to do something so immature. He'd always hated her hobby and reiterated that point when they last spoke. But she wouldn't confront him this time. The less she saw of him, the better.

"Your missing drawing." Becky closely examined the sketch. "Somehow I doubt that nasty X was there before."

"No. No, it wasn't."

"Did the cheating snake do that?"

"Who else?"

Christina went into the hotel room and placed it inside the wardrobe. The watercolor she'd done of him still lay on one of the shelves. She breathed a sigh of relief. But it couldn't stay there. She opened the middle drawer and placed the painting and the crumpled paper in, then closed it.

Becky walked toward the balcony. "I've got to finish eating and get ready to meet George at the beach in half an hour."

Christina followed her to the balcony's table and sat down. "You two sure love the beach."

Becky raised a brow. "Already forgot I'm part mermaid?"

She laughed. "No."

"You're too young for fog brain. Mush brain, maybe, but not fog brain." Becky winked.

Christina chuckled. "I know. But don't *you* forget I have a lot on my mind."

"I haven't forgotten your piling on worry over your hopeful future." She leaned over the table. "Let me see your nails. Are there any left?"

Christina slid her hands under her thighs and shook her head. "Don't be ridiculous. I don't bite my nails."

"Uh-huh. Then why are you hiding them?"

Christina pulled her hands from under her and clasped them in her lap. "No reason. Just playing with you." She flashed a weak smile. Becky was dredging up the past. She glanced down at her hands. So far so good. She wouldn't start that nervous habit from childhood that Becky had always thought was gross.

Becky shrugged and sat back. "Anyway, all this crazy fretting is why I keep pouring out advice so you avoid popping pills and a bland diet." She gave her a wide grin.

They ate the rest of their lunch in silence before getting ready to leave the hotel.

After Becky left, Christina pulled on an above-the-knee, navy-blue skort, a white sleeveless top, and her usual leather sandals. She bound her hair in a long ponytail. A few brushes with the mascara wand and light pink gloss finished off her makeup. To add to her ensemble, she spritzed on her perfume behind her ears, between her breasts, and on her wrists. She did this regularly for special occasions, and meetings with Nathan had become one of those. He was worth the extra effort.

A CHILL CREPT UP CHRISTINA'S SPINE AS SHE STRODE DOWN THE sidewalk toward the lookout. The same uneasy feeling she'd had yesterday of someone following her had returned. She glanced behind her a few times while weaving through swarms of tourists. Nobody stood out. Nobody looked familiar. Justin didn't appear. Maybe it was all in her mind. She'd worried over Justin too much lately.

Christina shook off her nervousness and headed into the field of wildflowers.

Nathan was already sitting at the precipice when she arrived. He'd set up his easel and other art media. She sat next to him, and he turned toward her.

She smiled. "Hi. How did the visit with your friend go?"

"Good. But not half as good as this." He leaned over and gave her a soft kiss.

Their lips parted, and Christina chuckled. "I hope not."

He grinned at her, then pointed at his blank canvas. "A few windmills from over there…," he said, moving his finger toward the right side of the caldera, "are my subjects today."

"Nice." Christina pulled out her sketchbook and pencil from her art bag.

"How about you?"

She scanned the magnificent landscape and spotted a whitewashed home with several flowerpots and veils of bougainvillea hanging from the second-story balcony. "Flowers. Tons of them." She opened her book to a clean sheet of paper.

"Sounds good." He squeezed tubes of paint, adding small amounts to his palette. "You going to paint them with your watercolors afterward?"

"Oh yes."

They were quiet for a while as they began their projects.

Nathan broke the silence. "By the way, you look beautiful today."

Warmth flooded Christina's cheeks and belly, and she smiled coyly. "Thank you."

He leaned toward her again and inhaled. "Smell amazing too." His stunning blue eyes sparkled.

She sniffed near his bronze neck, taking in the spicy, musky scent of him. "So do you."

He chuckled, and she joined him.

"Hey, Christina!"

Justin's horrible voice came from behind them. Christina winced. Why was he here? Was he really that dense or just an obstinate creep? She huffed. *Both.*

Nathan looked over his shoulder just as she did.

"What do you want?" she said.

Justin, in holey jeans, a blue T-shirt, and atrocious orange flip-flops approached her. Stopping a couple of feet away, he curled his lip and glared at Nathan.

She rolled her eyes. "We're busy, Justin, and we already had our talk yesterday."

"I told you I wasn't finished."

Nathan shot a stinging glower at Justin. His jaw twitched. He set down his palette and stood up.

She scrambled to her feet, grabbing Nathan's hand. "You're finished, Justin. I don't care what you have to say."

Justin's face flushed. "Why are you spilling our private stuff in front of this guy?"

"Go away, Justin." Christina squeezed Nathan's hand.

Nathan's face was stony, and he flexed and fisted his hands. "You heard her. She doesn't want you here. Scram."

"It's okay, Nathan," she whispered close to his ear.

Justin waved his hands about. "What's going on with you and him?"

"None of your business." Christina let go of Nathan's hand and gazed up at him. "Give me a minute."

Nathan glared at Justin, then turned his attention to her. "Okay, but if you need me, I'm here."

She nodded, stepped over to Justin, and waved for him to follow her. "Come on. Let's get this over with."

"Hey, we've got a history together. Quit treating me like garbage. Give me some respect."

They stopped at the sidewalk next to the grassy field.

She folded her arms across her chest. "Why? You never gave me any."

He held up his hands in a pathetic pleading gesture. "Look. I told you I made mistakes."

"Yes."

"Why can't you forgive me?"

"It's not a matter of forgiving, Justin."

"Then what is it?"

"I don't love you anymore." She shook her head. "Haven't loved you for the past two years."

"I'm not that man anymore." His hand cupped her shoulder. "It's still possible we can start fresh, and you can grow to love me again."

She moved from his touch. "Why would I want to do that?"

"Because I've learned from my mistakes. I'm a better man now."

"I don't think you have."

Justin sighed. "You're not giving me a chance to show you. I see you still have the habit of misinterpreting what I say. Open your mind and heart and listen to me. I'm here, made this long trip just to work things out with you."

Christina grimaced. *Misinterpreting what he says. His gaslighting continues.* "There's nothing to work out, Justin. Go back home." Christina pivoted on her heel and headed back to Nathan.

When she reached Nathan, she peered over her shoulder. Justin was marching toward his hotel. She blew out a breath. Thank God that was over. Maybe he'd actually leave the island now.

Nathan gathered her in his arms, and she leaned her cheek against his chest, comforted by his embrace.

They broke their hug, and he gazed down at her. "Would I be prying if I asked if you wanted to talk about what just happened?"

She lost herself in his beautiful, soft eyes. There was such solace inside her by his presence. If only Justin would really leave the island, then the peaceful feeling would be even more intense. For now, she'd have to accept that at least he wouldn't bother her again while here.

"Christina?" Nathan raised his hand and touched the side of her face.

She lowered her eyes. What would he think of her if she told him about her failed marriage? Her loss?

He gently ran a hand over her hair.

She locked gazes with him again, and her heart tightened.

A crease settled between his eyebrows. "You don't have to tell me. I just thought you might feel better if you did."

His kindness was like a warm, cozy blanket wrapped around her. She could tell him. It wasn't like he was her disapproving father.

She took his hand and led him to the cliff. They sat down together.

"I'll tell you."

"You don't have—"

She put a finger to his lips. "I want to."

He nodded. "Okay."

Christina took a deep breath and released it slowly while staring out at the sea, allowing herself to collect her thoughts. Rubbing her palms on her thighs, she turned to face Nathan. "That guy is my ex-husband."

Nathan's jaw slackened, but his eyes didn't leave hers.

She had to keep going to get through what she had to say. "We divorced nine months ago."

"That hasn't been very long."

"We were already having problems a couple of years before the divorce."

"What happened?"

"We were married five years. In our third year of marriage, I became pregnant."

Nathan bowed his head and clasped his hands in his lap.

She pressed forward. "I was so happy, and so was he."

"I'm sure." He gave her a small smile, his eyes reflecting a mixture of what looked like sorrow and comprehension.

Christina's hand instinctively went to her abdomen. "But it was short-lived."

Nathan frowned.

"I lost the baby in my fifth month."

His face drained of color, and a look of agony glistened in his eyes. He hugged her tightly. "I'm so sorry."

She hung on to him, wading through the waves of nostalgic pain.

When they finally released each other, Christina wiped away the wetness on her cheeks. "Our marriage went downhill from there."

Nathan held her hand in his and put his other on top of hers.

"I had a hard time getting over the loss of Anna."

Nathan's expression held so much compassion. "The name of your baby?"

She nodded and continued. "Spent many months numb and distant." She gazed at the horizon. "Justin lost patience with me and found someone else."

Nathan held her again, smoothing down her hair.

She hadn't expected complete and utter empathy from him. Some sympathy, yes, but his response was nearly overwhelming, as if he could feel what she felt and took on some of her pain.

She kissed his cheek and released him. "Thank you for listening and for the shoulder."

He touched her chin with his thumb. "Of course. You've been through so much. I'm glad to lend you a shoulder."

She smiled and kissed his hand.

Nathan rubbed her back as they looked out to sea.

Distant voices of people on the busy streets and Greek music drifting on the gentle breeze gave her solace.

He picked up his palette. "How about collaborating, artist?"

She grinned and picked up her sketchpad. "Upward and onward."

As he began to fill his canvas with tan outlines of the windmills, she secretly drew another picture of him, just as he was. Doing what he loved.

When they'd finished, they walked back to their hotel together, holding hands. They stopped in front of the door to her room.

Nathan laid his hands on either side of her waist and bent to kiss her. His soft lips pressed gently against hers before pulling away. "I'll see you tomorrow for the boat trip."

"I wouldn't miss it."

She watched him walk down the hall, his toned, tanned body moving with ease and strength. With a sigh, she went into her room, daydreaming about what tomorrow would bring.

Chapter Nineteen

Christina washed off her paintbrush in the bathroom sink, returned to the desk, and closed her watercolors container. The latest drawing of Nathan popped with vivid colors.

"You ready?" Becky asked, snapping her gum.

"In a minute. I need to set this out to dry before I can put it away."

"We're supposed to meet the guys in five minutes."

"Yes, I know."

"You're going to make us late, aren't you?" Becky grimaced.

"The lobby is only a couple of minutes from here."

"That's a yes then."

Christina blew on the painting. "Why don't you go, and I'll be there in a sec."

"You don't have to tell me twice." Becky winked, then slipped out the door.

Christina scanned the room. Where would be a safe place to stash the drawing? She made sure the balcony door's flimsy little lock was secured and left the sheet half under the small eave of the desk. It could still dry well enough there. She grabbed her purse and headed out of the room.

NATHAN LEANED AGAINST THE FRONT DESK, NEXT TO GEORGE AND Thalia.

Becky came down the stairs, gave a quick wave, and flashed a smile at them.

Nathan peered past Becky. "Where's Christina?"

She held up her hands. "Relax. She'll be here in a few. Had to finish up one of her masterpieces." The good-sized bubble Becky blew popped, echoing through the lobby.

George draped an arm around Becky. "Got a piece for me?" He stuck out his hand, palm up.

Becky dropped a wrapped block of gum into his hand.

"Thanks, Red."

"Sure."

Thalia moved next to Nathan. "Is Christina late a lot?"

Nathan folded his arms across his chest. "No. She hasn't been the few times we've met up."

Doubt seeped into his heart. Would she back out of the boat trip? He shook his head. Why would she do that? Yesterday she'd given no indication of not wanting to go. He was being an idiot again. He straightened his posture and slid his hands into his pockets.

The elevator doors opened, and Christina stepped out of it.

He let out a relieved breath and smiled. "There she is."

"Yes, I see." Thalia glanced at Christina, then looped her arm through Nathan's. "You ready to go?"

He felt her elbow lock with his as Christina approached.

"Sorry. I had to finish up a few things before coming down. Hope I'm not late."

Nathan grinned, his heartbeat escalating at the sight of her. "You're right on time."

"The cab's here, guys," George said, and holding Becky's hand, they headed out the lobby's front doors.

Thalia gently pulled on Nathan's arm. "Time to go."

Nathan looked at Thalia, then Christina. Christina raised her brows, her dark eyes questioning.

He held out his other hand. "Come on."

Christina took his hand, and he led both women to the taxi.

George and Becky squeezed in the front passenger seat, Becky sandwiched between the driver and George's bulky frame. Nathan slid in the back seat and settled in the middle, with Thalia and Christina flanking him. Christina leaned her elbow on the armrest and looked out her window. He glimpsed through the corner of his eye Thalia sitting with hands clasped in her lap, a tight smile on her face, as if her face was pasted in that position. Yeah. The air was frosty around him. The two women didn't seem to be hitting it off. He'd have to find a way to smooth that out once on the boat. The mention of that word made him nauseous. He dug in his pocket, pulled out a Dramamine patch, and put it on his arm.

They reached the harbor and got out of the vehicle. The strong wind made the water choppy and more menacing. Storm clouds hovered in the distance. How could this be? Santorini's summers were known for being dry and sunny. He scowled. Was this really a good time to be going out in the deep water?

He glanced at George, who was beaming, standing tall, his legs apart, arms crossed, staring out at the Aegean. Nathan kept his focus on the pier.

They'd rented a thirty-six-foot boat and hired a captain to steer the craft. Nathan had talked George into having a professional at the helm. If he'd not convinced George, his friend would have taken the place of the captain, and Nathan was nervous enough. George was no expert, no matter how much he blathered on about learning to steer his uncle's speed boat when he'd been in his teens.

As Nathan checked his watch, the vessel bounced over the rough sea toward the harbor. The captain had arrived a couple of minutes past their departure time. George caught the rope the captain threw on the second try. He wrapped it around one of the pier's poles.

Christina smoothed down her red-flowered white blouse against the wind. Beige shorts accentuated her hips and long, tan legs. Her leather sandals' straps wrapped around her perfect ankles. The large, round sunglasses she'd worn a few days ago covered her eyes. She threw her fluttering, raven hair off her shoulders.

Nathan sidled next to Christina, inhaling her familiar flowery scent.

Thalia came alongside him. "When do we get to go on boat?"

George and Becky had already boarded.

Pushing aside the start of vertigo tilting the water, boat, and everyone side to side, Nathan grimaced. The Dramamine would kick in soon. He'd be all right. "Now." He gestured Thalia and then Christina ahead of him.

"Come on, slowpoke!" Becky yelled from the rocking vessel.

"We're coming. Be patient, Beck!" Christina shouted back.

Nathan's stomach did a somersault. How long did it take for the Dramamine to start working? Not fast enough.

He groaned and climbed aboard, grabbing any handle or solid object he could find. He snatched up one of the life jackets lying on the curved bench at the stern and put it on as fast as he could. Letting out a sigh of relief, he snapped the last buckle together.

A canopy covered a table and two chairs in front him. He sat on the left side of the long bench with the awning only partially covering him. He looked at the sky. The huge gray cloud was getting closer to them. He swallowed and turned toward George, who was standing a few feet away with hands on hips and a stupid grin on his face, as if he were the captain.

Nathan wagged an arm at his friend, then pointed at the sky. "Do you see the gigantic rain cloud?"

George glanced at it and shrugged. "Yeah. So?"

"Maybe this wasn't the best time to take a ride."

"Don't be a chicken—"

"Shut up, Moose!" Nathan looked around, making sure nobody heard what George had said.

George frowned. "Chill, man. You're trembling."

Nathan stiffened and wiped his sweaty palms on his shorts.

Christina stepped toward the bench, but Thalia slid in next to Nathan, a satisfied smile on her face. Christina frowned and moved toward the other side of the bench and sat, her face stoic, her eyes on the water. Barely able to control his panic, Nathan had failed to sit between the women like he'd planned.

George untied the rope and pushed the craft from the edge of the pier.

Nathan gritted his teeth as the boat swayed under the rolling waves.

The captain lifted a hand from the pilothouse of the craft as it motored away from the harbor.

Sweat beaded on Nathan's forehead. He gripped the metal and wood railing running behind the bench and sides of the stern.

"We're on our way to the hot springs there," the captain shouted above the wind and engine and pointed to the cove about a half a mile away.

The women put on their life jackets while George wandered around the deck as if he owned the boat.

The captain jutted his chin toward George. "You need life jacket too."

"Nope. I'm fine."

"But it was deal to be on boat."

George scowled, puffing out his chest. "I'll put it on soon."

The captain grimaced and turned back to steering the boat as it rocked through the contentious waves.

Thalia gave Nathan a smile similar to a cat that had eaten a mouse. "This is fun, no?"

He jerked a nod as he let go of the metal bar next to him, feigning confidence. "Sure is."

Christina moved from her spot on the bench and sat in the chair at the table, across from Becky. She now faced him at an angle, her eyes darting from him to Thalia every so often. Was she angry at him for not sitting with her? What could he do? He was stuck, feeling glued to his seat, not wanting to add any more movement to the deck. He gazed up at the sky. The storm cloud loomed overhead. The wind blew even harder as rain began to fall, pelting his skin. *Damn.* He should have gotten under the awning, sat at the table, away from the boat's edge.

Thalia raised her face skyward, letting the raindrops splash on her. She leaned back as the rain soaked her. "What joy. Never seen rain in summer here. This is wonderful!" she yelled over the pattering of the rain and the whoosh of the boat swaying violently on the rough water.

Nathan gripped the metal bar again and stole a look at Christina. She was leaning her forearms on the table, talking to Becky. George ducked under the canopy and squatted next to Becky. Nathan couldn't hear what they were saying. Thunder rumbled as the rain became a noisy downpour, competing with the crashing cacophony of the sea. The rocky formations surrounding the hot springs were about a quarter of a mile away.

The boat's motor stopped, and the captain poked his head out of the pilothouse. "We stop here. We cannot go closer to rocks and will wait here till storm pass. Not too long." He held the brim of his sailor cap, bowing his head, then moved back into the enclosure.

George crept out from under the covered area and leaned over the railing next to Nathan. He gaped and pointed at the water. "Look! Some big-ass fish!" He smacked Nathan on his padded shoulder, continuing to point.

The boat tilted deeply to the left. Nathan kept hold of the railing while Thalia slid down the bench to the other end, laughing. Christina and Becky held on to the bolted-down table as seawater sprayed over them. They were all soaked through, hair smashed to their heads and shoulders.

What a tour. Could it get any worse? Nathan ran a hand over his wet face, his vision blurred for a moment from the rain.

George nudged him again. "Look! Maybe it's a seal or something!"

With all the women's eyes on him, Nathan stood on unsteady legs. His muscles tightened as he tried to gain some semblance of equilibrium against the constant lurching of the boat. He took a breath, let it out, then forced himself to look at the deep water. Dizziness set in, and not only was the craft bouncing about through the now lighter rain, but he was sure his head was ready to spin off his body. His heart thumped in his chest, and he breathed hard out of his mouth.

The boat took a hard pitch to the right side, leaning heavily toward the rolling, crushing waves, as one splashed a waterfall over him and George. He caught his breath, trying to steady himself. But the rocking and dizziness only got worse.

Reaching for the metal bar to his right, he slipped on the wet floor of the deck and plummeted off the side of the boat into the cold, monstrous water, one of its waves barreling over him. Saltwater rushed into his gaping mouth and into his nose. His heart was ready to jump out of his chest.

As soon as he'd popped back up out of the cursed sea swell, he coughed out the water, his throat scratchy and sore, as terror struck him so hard his body went rigid, paralyzed. He huffed and puffed, gasping for air and floated helplessly in the endless rise and fall of the waves.

The childhood memory of him sinking helplessly into the cloudy lake jolted him. His teeth chattered and body trembled as he fought to erase the image in his mind.

He wiped his eyes. The boat swayed on the rough water a dozen feet away. The women were lined up on the bench, watching, but he couldn't make out their faces. In the midst of the chilly, salty water, shame and embarrassment warmed his wet cheeks while he shook with fear. God, he wanted to die right there.

George appeared at the stern, throwing on his life jacket. He dove into the water. His friend swam toward him in quick strokes, fighting against the raging waves. Nathan noticed the boat had drifted toward the rocky area where the hot springs were located, maybe thirty feet away. If he could move, maybe he could climb onto those jagged stones, out of the cursed water.

George's hand clasped Nathan's life vest around his shoulder. He swam closer to him, turning him around, facing the boat. An unruly wave swept them back toward the rocks, causing Nathan to slam his padded back against his friend. George's grip lessened on his life jacket, then fell away. Nathan struggled to turn around. George's eyes were closed, mouth ajar, his head leaning back against his lifted life vest. Splotches of blood colored the rock behind his head and slid down George's neck as he bobbed on the surface of the water. Swirling sea slammed against the rocks and poured over George's face.

Nathan flailed about, his heart pounding in his ears. "Jesus! George!" He shot his hands out, grasping for George's body.

Something tugged on his life jacket. He glanced behind him. Becky let go of him, darted the few feet to George, and put her arm around his neck. She swam as if she had the strength of ten men, pulling George toward the boat that had moved several feet in Nathan's direction.

Becky lifted George's hulky body toward the captain and Thalia, leaning over the opening in the stern. They pulled him into the boat as Becky swam back to Nathan. She reached him and gazed up at the sky. The rain had stopped. She then grabbed hold of his life vest over his shoulder and pulled him toward the boat. "Come on, bud. You're okay."

He wiggled his arms and legs in an attempt to copy her moves, concentrating on her orange life jacket instead of the endless waves slapping against the sides of his face. He was okay. She was bringing him back to the craft. Nothing to worry about. He'd be okay.

A wave crested and slammed over him, and he bobbed back up a minute later, choking on salt water. His beating heart raced again as he gasped for air.

Becky continued to drag him forward. His left shoulder hit the back of the boat. Two hands reached for him. He blindly thrust up his arms, then gazed up into Christina's pale face, her dark eyes shining with distress. She grabbed hold of his arms as he clutched the metal railing of the short ladder attached to the back of the vessel. Becky pushed him from behind. Thalia appeared next to Christina just as he climbed into the boat.

Thalia and the captain guided him to the bench and had him lie down. His chest heaved, and he coughed the last of the salt water from his mouth. Once his breathing calmed, he turned his head toward George on the deck floor near the table, the captain setting a towel under his head. *Shit. Is he dead?* Nathan tried to sit up, but Christina sat by his head and laid a hand on his chest.

"He's okay." She raised her head toward the captain. "He stopped the bleeding, did CPR, and got all the water out of George's lungs."

Nathan let out a long sigh of relief, then tensed. George still hadn't opened his eyes. Christina smoothed down Nathan's hair and gazed down at him with knitted brows.

Thalia sat by Nathan's feet. She pulled on his arm, helping him to sit up slowly. She patted his shoulder and gave him a friendly smile. "The captain is taking us back to harbor so they can take George to hospital."

Nathan nodded and looked toward the pier getting closer by the minute. Relief swept over him as the boat docked, and he and the others disembarked. His legs were wobbly, and the cement harbor seemed to rock a bit before he got his bearings. But he soon steadied himself and removed his life jacket.

The captain had jogged over to a cab sitting by the travel agency building. The taxi rolled over to them, and Nathan helped Becky and the captain load George into the back seat.

Becky hopped in the front seat and shot an arm through the open window. "We'll be at the Santorini Hospital's ER! I'll send back the cab!"

The car sped from the harbor and up the zig-zagged road toward Thira.

Soaking wet, Nathan watched his friend go, then looked to his left and right. Christina and Thalia flanked him.

Christina's beautiful, damp hair whipped around like the feathery wings of a blackbird. She gently wrapped her arms around his neck and gazed into his eyes. Despite the chilly wind against his wet body, heat flowed through him.

"You scared me back there."

He didn't know what to say, but she didn't seem to want an answer, hugging him and leaning her cheek against his.

But he couldn't ignore he'd made a total fool of himself on that boat. He should've stayed seated, but George had insisted he look at a stupid fish or whatever it was in that deep, deadly water. The whole event rolled through his mind like the waves that had crashed against him. He shook his head. Christina released him, ran a hand over the side of his face, then stepped back as Thalia moved toward him.

"George be okay. We see him soon."

"Yeah." Was George really all right? He'd still been unconscious when the captain and Becky hauled him off the craft and he'd helped them settle George in the cab. How well did that captain know CPR?

His best friend had tried to save his life. He gritted his teeth. The whole outing had been a disaster, a mistake, just as he thought it would be. But George never listened. Would he recover to learn from this near-death experience?

Nathan shivered from the wind battering his damp clothes against his body. He gazed at the cluster of white buildings sitting on the top of the caldera. He wouldn't dwell on terrible thoughts about George and would wait to see for himself that his friend was all right.

Chapter Twenty

I n the cab ride to the hospital, Christina laced her fingers with Nathan's. She peeked past him. Thalia was looking out her window. *Good.* Nathan's friend had come off as a third wheel. But Christina had let it go since Nathan and Thalia were good friends from childhood. Their relationship seemed like brother and sister, and that was fine with her.

The harrowing boat trip came back to her. Nathan falling out of the boat, his face pale and broadcasting complete terror, swirled in her head. Her heart had nearly stopped. After witnessing his flailing about in the rough water, she'd come to the realization he didn't know how to swim. Fear for him had sat in the pit of her stomach, but she'd been locked in place. Even though she could swim fairly well, the unruly sea didn't give her confidence to attempt to be a hero. Thank God for Becky and her excellent swimming skills. She'd saved both men. She smiled at the irony.

"We here," the taxi driver said.

"Thanks." Nathan paid him.

They got out of the car and went through the ER's doors. Nathan checked in at the front desk, then they followed a nurse down the hall.

They went inside a room separated by a curtain between the

beds. George lay in the first one, and Becky sat by him, patting his chest.

George's weary face lit up at the sight of Nathan. "Hey, Nate."

Nathan approached George and put a hand on his beefy shoulder. "I'm glad to see you awake. How are you feeling?"

"I'm fine." He lifted himself on his elbows and groaned, placing his hand on the back of his head. "Head doesn't feel too great, but how long can a headache last? And when can I get out of here?"

Christina folded her arms and suppressed a smile. *George always thinking he was invincible. Wait until he finds out who the real invincible one is.* She held in a chuckle, casting an admirable glance at Becky.

Becky pressed her hand against his shoulder. "Lie down and rest, silly. We've got to wait for the CAT scan results."

"Why'd they do that? I don't need—"

"You don't remember whacking your head on the rocks, do you?" Becky said.

George's mouth hung open as his stare traveled around the room. "No. I only remember swimming to Nathan."

"You were unconscious for a while," Nathan said.

"Becky saved you," Christina said and gave a nod toward Becky, who never disappointed anyone with what she was capable of.

"Yes, Becky save you," Thalia added, giving Becky a look akin to envy.

Christina wondered if Thalia's skin tone would turn a hue of green at any minute. Who wouldn't be jealous of Becky's talents? Christina laughed to herself.

George's brows lifted.

Becky shrugged. "You know I'm a mermaid."

A big grin spread across George's face. "Yeah. The prettiest one ever." His face turned pink. "Thanks."

Becky squeezed his hand.

A short, stocky doctor with thinning hair came in with a tablet.

"Hello, Mr. Panos. I'm Doctor Soulis. We have the results of your CT scan, and it appears you have a concussion."

"Concussion?" George repeated with a grimace.

"Yes. You'll need to stay for a few more hours to be monitored. Then you can go home. But"—the doctor held up a finger—"you'll need someone to watch you tonight and the night after to make sure you're okay."

"Aww, I don't need anybody to watch—"

"The doctor just said you do. Now shut up and follow his orders," Nathan scolded before flashing a grin.

"I can stay with him, if you'd like," Becky said, looking over at Nathan.

George beamed. "That works for me."

Nathan pointed at George. "Looks like you'll be in better company than me."

"He must rest for at least five days," the doctor said.

"Five days?" George tried to sit up again, but Becky and Nathan pushed on his shoulders until he lay back against the mattress and pillow. "That's a lot of wasted vacation days."

"Not with me, they aren't." Becky winked at him.

Christina laughed under her breath. Becky would be busy for the next few nights. She'd have the hotel room to herself. She peered at Nathan and tapped a finger to her chin. *Hmm.* Maybe this would give them more time to spend together.

George closed his eyes and smiled. "Okay. This whole rest thing just got better."

Christina ran a hand over her damp top. She needed a shower. She touched Nathan's arm. "I'll see you back at the hotel."

"Yeah. I need to go back and clean up too."

Thalia's stare darted around the room. "I go also."

Christina frowned. Why couldn't she stay at the hospital or go back to her hotel on her own? She hoped Thalia wouldn't try to monopolize the precious time left on the island Christina planned to spend with Nathan.

Becky waved. "See you guys later."

Outside the hospital, Christina climbed into a cab with Nathan and Thalia. The driver dropped Thalia off near her hotel. Christina exhaled as soon as the woman disappeared inside the building, thankful Thalia wasn't sharing the same hotel as her and Nathan.

The driver dropped them off at their hotel. They entered the cool lobby, a chill running through her. They got into the elevator, and Nathan kissed her. "I need to go back to the hospital after I shower and work out the plans with George tonight. With Becky staying, we'll need to change our sleeping arrangements. See you tomorrow?"

Maybe they could play musical beds? While Becky stayed with George, Nathan could sleep in Becky's bed. Her cheeks burned at the thought. Little Father Apostolos came to mind. What about her virtuous plans to be a nun? How could she be thinking in such carnal ways when she'd been so set on becoming a nun when she'd flown here and even visited the abbess at the museum only a few days ago?

Nathan embraced her tightly and kissed her neck. "Okay?"

Christina shook away the confusion in her head and smiled. "Yes."

The doors opened. Nathan squeezed her hand before they left the elevator and headed down the hall.

He strode a couple of doors down from the elevator and waved at her as she glanced back, heading toward her room, alone. She stiffened and fisted her hands. *Stop it. Clean out that dirty mind of yours. Your path isn't clear yet.* Even as she said this to herself, the pull toward Nathan caused her abdomen to fill with an aching warmth.

She entered her room and fell on her bed. *Don't let yourself go that far, no matter what Becky told you.* She went to the shower and turned it on, preparing to immerse herself in the steaming hot water.

Fresh and clean both in mind and body, Christina came out of the bathroom wearing shorts and a T-shirt. She went to the desk where her drawing still lay. She nodded. Locking the balcony's door may have saved her latest work.

A few ripples ran down the stiff paper from the dried paint. She stored it in the wardrobe on the second shelf.

A knock came at the door. Her stomach knotted at the thought of Justin standing on the other side of the door. Another rap came.

She wasn't going to be bullied. Justin or not, she would answer. Pulling the door open, she found Maria there with Dino next to her, his teeth flashing through his beard. Relief loosened the tightness in her belly.

"Hey, cousin."

"Hi. Come in." Christina moved to the side.

Maria and Dino entered the room.

"I wanted to invite you to Dino's friend's restaurant for an early dinner," Maria said, then flicked her finger back and forth between her and Dino. "We leave in the morning, and I wanted to spend some time with you before then."

"Sounds great." Christina looked down at her attire. "Is this okay, or do I need to upgrade the clothes?"

Maria waved a hand in dismissal, her mouth turned slightly down in an appraising expression. "Nah. That works just fine."

"Okay. I'll grab my purse, and we can go."

This would be a good way to spend the evening, keeping her mind—as much as was possible—off Nathan until tomorrow.

Chapter Twenty-One

Christina, Maria, and Dino entered the sparsely populated restaurant and bar. The locals didn't eat dinner at five o'clock, and Christina enjoyed having the quietness and space largely to themselves. They took their seats at a table a few feet from the wide bar with its ten stools.

"How's the vacation been going?" Maria asked.

"Pretty well." She didn't feel the need to mention the boating mishap. "How about yours?"

"It's been great." She looked at Dino. "Hasn't it?"

Dino nodded. "Yup."

A waiter showed up, setting a basket of sliced bread and glasses of water on the table.

"Do you want to share the calamari and dolmades platter?" Maria asked.

"Sure."

"A couple of beers for us," Maria said, pointing to her and Dino.

"A glass of white wine would be fine for me," Christina said.

The waiter nodded and left their table.

"What do you think of Dino's friend's place?" Maria gestured, as if she were Vanna White.

"It's really nice."

Dino beamed. "It's the best restaurant on the island."

A few more people entered the building and found a table. Christina scanned the room with its white walls cluttered with posters of the Greek islands, boats, and random items—sailor hats, fishing nets, starfish, and a large anchor. Instrumental Greek music streamed through the room. An easel holding a placard said in both Greek and English, LIVE MUSIC EVERY TUESDAY, THURSDAY, AND SATURDAYS AFTER 8 P.M. Christina would be in her hotel room before eight. She couldn't imagine enjoying the entertainment without Nathan. She bit her lip. Boy, she couldn't stop thinking about him. It was safer for her to just return to her room for the night after dinner and catch up on reading one of her books.

"Christina," Maria said, touching her hand.

Christina turned her attention to her cousin.

"We're thinking of moving here and working in Telly's restaurant."

"Wow. What a great opportunity." Christina squeezed Maria's hand. "I'm happy for you."

Maria grinned and patted Dino's arm. "We're thinking late August."

"That's wonderful." Christina noticed Maria and Dino gazing into each other's eyes. He'd definitely become more than a friend.

The waiter arrived with the food and set it in the middle of the table. "Enjoy," he said and walked off.

They ate in silence for a few minutes before Maria said, "I got the info really late, but I still need to tell you. I'm sorry about the loss of your baby... your divorce." Her eyes and mouth drooped in sympathy.

"Thank you." She didn't want to think about that and focused on her food.

"I hope you find someone who will treat you better and really appreciate you." Maria grabbed a piece of pita bread, then looked at her. "You deserve it."

Christina nodded with her mouth full of spanakopita. That someone could be Nathan. The signs were glowing toward him lately, but there were still mixed signals about her plans. She pursed her lips together. *Keep focused on Maria and the delicious food.* "Thanks."

She glanced toward the bar. Half the stools were now occupied, the people's backs facing her. One of the men's backsides looked too familiar, with the faded jeans, T-shirt, and those gaudy orange flip-flops. Her appetite waned as her stomach twisted.

Justin.

He had his arm around a blonde with a floral miniskirt and tight black top. Three-inch black sandals completed her outfit. She laughed at whatever Justin was telling her.

Typical Justin. All those tiring explanations of his changing had been a lie, just as she'd thought. But finding him with the woman at the bar took away her stomachache. Finally he'd leave her alone. And if he was going to be sticking around that woman, she didn't care if he stayed on the island. He was out of her hair. That was all that mattered.

Justin turned his head to look at the blonde, but his stare traveled to Christina. A mischievous smile split his face, and he waved at her. She grimaced, hoping he wouldn't come to her table. She didn't want a scene. He faced the bar again.

She breathed easily and went back to eating and enjoying the last hour with her cousin.

THE ROOM WAS SO QUIET; IT WAS DEAFENING WITHOUT BECKY THERE. But at the same time, it was nice having the place to herself. Christina wouldn't keep Becky up reading like she unintentionally usually did. She certainly wasn't allowing the idea of Nathan sleeping in Becky's bed or even slipping into hers back into her thoughts. She'd stand firm, concentrating on discovering her purposeful road ahead.

After lighting the handful of vanilla-scented candles on the desk, she lay in bed and picked up her book *The Unlikely Pilgrimage of Harold Fry*, delving into his world.

An hour later her eyelids drooped. She closed the book, set it on the nightstand, and turned off the lamp. She rolled onto her side and cuddled under the covers. Smiling, she closed her eyes and fell into a restful slumber.

A hand covered her mouth, abruptly jerking her out of sleep. Her eyes sprang open to darkness, but her mouth was still blocked. Her heartbeat galloped in her chest. She screamed against the hand, the sound coming out a low, muffled noise.

"Calm down. It's just me." Justin's voice floated over her shoulder.

The heat of his body behind hers made her nauseous. She ripped his hand from her mouth and sat up with a jolt. "What the hell are you doing in here?" She pressed a hand to her chest, working to calm herself.

Justin lay on his side, his elbow resting on the pillow, his cheek leaning on his hand. He smiled at her as if his middle-of-the-night creepy appearance was completely normal.

She got out of her bed and slid into Becky's. "How'd you get into my room?"

He jutted his chin toward the balcony door cracked open.

"That was locked."

"Chintzy lock."

Christina folded her arms across her chest. "You'd know all about chintzy."

He ran a hand over the sheet. "Had to come by and make sure you were okay after seeing me at the restaurant."

"Why wouldn't I be?"

"I don't want you to get the wrong idea."

Christina raised her brows. Where was he going with this? She was half-interested in what tale he'd make up.

"I ran into her there at the bar. It was no big deal. Just friendly talk."

"Uh-huh."

"So, you didn't think I'd given up on us."

She pursed her lips. "I was hoping you had."

Justin crawled out of the bed and moved toward Becky's.

Christina put up a hand. "Stay there."

He shrugged and sat on the edge of her bed.

"Go with the woman at the bar. I don't care. I told you we were done two years ago."

"You won't get me back talking that way."

"Good."

His face flushed. "You know, she treats me a whole hell of a lot better than you."

"Good."

He put his fists on his thighs and glowered at her. "This is your last chance. I'm not going to keep begging."

"Good."

"Stop saying that!"

Christina sighed. "Justin, I'm never coming back to you. Accept it and go on with your life. You'll find someone who fits with you."

His face fell, and his eyes softened. This time Christina believed he'd finally gotten the message. Maybe if she'd just been that gentle instead of combative the first time, he would have gotten it. Either way, defeat and acceptance showed in his eyes.

Justin stood, straightened his shirt, and lifted his chin. "Okay. Don't say I didn't try. I *will* find someone who'll respect and appreciate me."

"Good."

He opened his mouth as if to respond to her, but instead, he pivoted on his heel, sauntered to the door, and left the room.

The door clicked shut, like the permanent closing of an old chapter in her life. She got up and closed the balcony door, turning the flimsy lock. At this point, she didn't need to worry about the *chintzy* lock now that Justin had gone for good. Sighing, she slid back into her bed, turned on the lamp, and picked up her book.

Chapter Twenty-Two

Midafternoon, Nathan sat at a desk in his uncle's office, creating a memorable likeness of his yiayia with his paintbrush. He planned to have it completed before he left the island and went to visit his papou in Athens.

This newest work of his would be a surprise for Papou, and he imagined his grandfather's eyes sparkling and face lighting up when he set his eyes on the vivid painting of Yiayia.

The loss of Yiayia fourteen years ago had been painful, never to feel her gentle hugs or taste her amazing homemade *stefado* again. Papou had been devastated. Pneumonia had taken Yiayia, and Papou had never been the same. How could he be?

Nathan dabbed his thin brush in yellow paint and dotted the petals of daffodils on the white surface of the painting, above green stems shooting out of an oval-shaped, glass vase. They were his grandmother's favorite flower. They bloomed around Pascha, Yiayia's favorite holiday. He grabbed another brush and finished Yiayia's powder-blue dress. She sat on a chair next to the table with the daffodils, her hands clasped in her lap, a hint of a smile on her olive-skinned face.

"Ah, Nathan, my boy, you painting something of your own."

Thío Ioannis stood at the arched opening, hands pressed

against each side. He gave him a wide grin, then sauntered over. He studied the painting. "Despina. You make her as beautiful as she was in person."

"Thanks, *Thío*."

"It for your papou?"

"Yes."

He nodded. "Good. He will like very much." *Thío* Ioannis slapped him on the back.

Nathan smiled as he finished up Yiayia's black shoes.

His uncle tapped his shoulder. "My boy, you already finish mural and these walls." He gestured toward the blue-and-white walls.

"Yes, just a little while ago before working on this."

"You so fast."

"You know how much I love painting. I could spend all day on it."

Thío Ioannis's face lit up, and he waved his arms. "You should sell your work. It go for big bucks."

Nathan laughed. "I don't know about that."

His uncle nudged his arm. "Hey, you smiling a lot. Something change with you?"

"What do you mean?" He did feel great, even after the disastrous boat trip. He'd been floating the past few days. No life jacket required. Being around Christina gave him buoyancy. Made his heart grow three times bigger.

"Tell me." *Thío* Ioannis said, patting Nathan on the chest. "The girl who came to see you the other day. She take your heart?"

Nathan's cheeks burned.

"Aha!" His uncle chuckled and shook him. "You find special girl like I said you would."

He set down his paints. "I might have."

"Might?" *Thío* Ioannis gently smacked his cheek. "I know that look. It's love."

Nathan left the stool and held up his hands. "Okay, okay."

Thío Ioannis gave him a bear hug, then pointed at him. "I pay you for your fantastic work."

Nathan followed his uncle out of the room. "You don't have to do that."

Thío Ioannis swung around with hands raised. "Don't be a crazy man. You earned it."

He smiled as his uncle pulled out money from below the counter and handed it to him. "Thank you."

"Take your girl to dinner."

Nathan put the wad of bills in his pocket. "I will. But first I've got to clean up my mess in your office."

"Okay. I agree with that." His uncle winked.

He headed back to the little room and gathered up his brushes. Washing them off at the bathroom sink, he pictured Christina at the precipice. Maybe they'd have another art collaboration soon, but dinner sounded good. He'd make sure to ask her when he got back to the hotel.

He collected his painting, pochade, and left the room, heading toward the front of the store.

His uncle snapped his fingers. "Does your girlfriend like fishing?"

"I don't know. And she's not my—"

"You find out. It may be only way I get you to go fishing with me." He chuckled.

Nathan laughed. "Sure." But his heart sank. How many pleas to go fishing had his uncle made? If only he knew how to swim a little, even just float. Maybe he wouldn't be so afraid of the water and could get on his uncle's small boat and fulfill his dream.

A few hours later, Christina nearly ran into Nathan in the hotel's lobby. Perfect timing. An idea had sprouted early in the morning, and she wanted to find him and tell him as soon as possible.

"Just the person—" she began.

"I've been looking for," Nathan said.

"You too?" She smiled and wrapped her arms around his neck.

He moved his bag to the side and curled an arm around her waist. His lips met hers in a quick kiss. "I need to drop off my bag."

"Good." She ran her fingers through his thick, dark hair. "You can throw on your swim trunks while you're at it."

His body stiffened against hers, and he stepped back, letting out a nervous laugh, his dimples gleaming. "I don't—"

She took his hand and guided him to the elevator. "I know you don't know how to swim."

His face turned pink.

Christina kissed his colored cheek. "I'm going to teach you to swim."

The doors opened, and she pulled Nathan into the elevator.

He scrunched his face. "I don't know…"

"Don't worry. I have a small pool on my balcony. It's the perfect depth and size for practicing."

He didn't look convinced, tilting his head to the side and opening his mouth to speak.

She put a finger to his lips. "Didn't I just say don't worry?"

"Kinda hard not to."

The doors opened, and they headed to his room. Christina pointed at the door. "You go ahead and get changed, and I'll do the same."

His beautiful blue eyes darkened, and a smile tugged at the corner of his mouth.

She giggled and hurried toward her room.

Once inside, she stripped off her clothes and pulled on her black swimsuit, grabbed a towel, and went out on the balcony. She set the towel on one of the chairs and gazed out at the beautiful golden-orange sun. The weather was perfect for a dip in the pool.

Several minutes passed, and she wondered if he'd decided not to come. She paced the floor, biting her lip until two knocks sounded. She raced over and opened the door.

Nathan looked at her like a lost puppy, a towel draped around his neck. He wore blue swim trunks and those Apostle-like sandals. Her heart fluttered while her body melted like warm wax. But she quickly snapped out of it, pulled him inside the room, then pointed to the pool.

"It's right over there."

He stared at the water as if it were lava. "Yeah. I see it."

Christina laughed. "Don't worry. I won't let anything happen to you." She slid a hand across his hairy chest. "Besides, you can touch the bottom in there. It's five feet deep, and aren't you about six feet or so?"

He nodded before cocking his head to the side, as if evaluating the situation.

She took his hand and led him to the three steps that descended into the water. He squeezed her hand tightly. She winced. "Try not to cut off my circulation, eh?"

"Oh, sorry." Nathan loosened his grip.

"Thanks." She lowered herself into the water, a little at a time until she was waist-deep, then sank into the water, lapping over her shoulders. She let out a squeal. "It's a little cold but refreshing."

He frowned, gazing down at her.

Poor thing. He needed reassurance.

She moved toward the stairs and held out her hand. "Go ahead and take off your shoes, then hold my hand."

He did so and grasped her outstretched hand, looking down at the water as if it would swallow him whole. "Promise me you know what you're doing."

"I think I do."

He put his foot on the first step, giving her a look of disapproval, his jaw tight. "You think."

"I've never really done this before—"

"Okay." He let go of her hand, swiveled around, and stepped out of the pool.

Why did you say that, dummy? Ugh. She bit her lip and looked up at him. "Can you try to trust me on this?"

He casted a sideways glance at her, full of doubt.

"I can at least teach you to float."

His eyes widened.

She'd said something that registered. She exhaled in relief.

His expression softened. "I want to learn that."

"Good. Come on." She held out her hand again, and he took it.

Nathan walked down the three steps and stood next to her, his breathing heavy, his stare flitting about. He didn't let go of her hand, squeezing it.

She directed him to hold on to one of the pool's sides.

"Okay."

She let go of the hand she held and set it on the lip of the pool as well.

He held on to the side as if he were going to be swept away even though the surface of the water was just below his neck. "Don't go anywhere."

"I wasn't planning to."

"Good."

She chuckled and touched his muscular back. "So, I'm going to have you try to lift your legs off the floor and kick them back and forth."

He looked at her over his shoulder, as if she were asking him to fly.

"Just try it." She tapped the pool's edge with the palm of her hand. "Remember, you're still holding on. You're in control."

"Okay." He attempted to lift his feet but bounced back down. "It's not working."

She slipped her arms under his stomach. "You need to push against the floor and lift your legs behind you, then start kicking."

He tried several times and eventually got his legs to kick more than twice.

"Great. You're making progress."

"Doesn't feel like it."

"Well, you are." She kept her arms under his chest as he continued to practice the pushing off and kicking.

Twenty minutes later, he'd loosened his grip on the pool's side and trusted her to hold him up, being weightless in the water.

She lowered her arms a few inches and allowed him to float above them. "You're doing it, Nathan!" Her muscles tightened with excitement as she lightly bounced on the balls of her feet.

He coughed as water splashed off his cheeks and mouth.

"Keep it up."

With one last gasp, he got out a few more kicks before setting his feet on the floor.

She came alongside him and rested her elbow on the edge. "It's a good start."

He wiped his wet face and nodded.

"Once you get that down, treading water is the next important thing to learn." She pushed wet hair off her shoulder.

"Isn't that floating in place?"

"Yes. If you can do that for long periods of time, you'll be in good shape if you're ever in an emergency."

She lowered herself in the water and showed him how it was done. He watched with interest, the corners of his mouth slightly lifting in appreciation.

"Now you try." Christina stood and leaned her back against the side of the pool.

He attempted her moves over and over before waving his arms, splashing her. "I give up."

"There's no giving up in treading water, Nathan." She grinned.

He rolled his eyes.

"Give it another try."

Nathan wiggled about for the next thirty minutes, reaching success in the last few moments.

"Great job!"

He panted as if he'd swum the English Channel.

She glided toward him and put her arms around his shoulders. "You were amazing."

A smile she hadn't seen since he'd gotten into the water lit up his face. "I did it, didn't I?"

"Yes, you did."

She pressed her mouth against his, and their kiss deepened, their tongues exploring. Warmth spread through her, her abdomen aching with desire. Holding on to him, she lifted her legs and wrapped them around his waist. He gaped, falling back against the steps, landing on the second one, with water rolling off his chest. Her legs were still locked around him, and her lips found his again, joining in another sensuous, sweet encounter.

Distant Greek music drifted in the air, with the smell of the sea tickling her nose as she held on to Nathan, her heart thudding in her chest, her body like warm fudge syrup. She sighed against his mouth, then rubbed her cheek against his stubbly one.

His hands traveled up and down her back. She arched in response, and he nibbled on her ear.

She was lost in his arms, the feel of his soft lips on her neck, the muffled sound of the door shutting only barely heard.

"Christina?"

Becky's voice.

Christina let go of Nathan and scrambled off his lap as he swung around to face Becky approaching them. He sank down, landing on the bottom step so that the water covered his stomach, hiding his lower half, his cheeks glowing pink. Christina suppressed a smile, her own face warming.

"Looks like the private swim's been going, shall we say, swimmingly." Becky winked and popped her gum.

"Ha ha," Christina sputtered, then grinned sheepishly at her friend.

"It's a good thing you told me your plans so I could find you easily."

Christina folded her arms. "Now I wish I hadn't told you."

Becky chuckled. "I bet."

"So, what's the emergency that you had to interrupt our lesson?"

"Lesson. Hmm." Becky eyed her and Nathan before she gave them a knowing smile.

Christina's face flamed once more.

"Well, I hate to break up your important *work*, but George is asking for you, Nathan. Wants you to play some video game with him." She shook her head, blowing a bubble. It snapped loudly.

Nathan stood and put his hands on his hips. "Really?"

"Yeah, I know. It's nutty, but that's George."

"Can't he play with you?"

"I'm not into video games, bud."

"Can't he play by himself?"

Becky lowered her chin, giving Nathan a chiding expression. "He's laid up and bored, remember?"

Nathan scratched his cheek. "Your company isn't good enough?"

"I know, right?" Becky rolled her eyes. "What an insult."

"His timing sucks," Nathan grumbled, then turned toward Christina and embraced her.

She held him and whispered in his ear, "It's okay. You know where I am."

Becky headed toward the door. "I'll tell him you'll be there in a few." She left the room.

He ran a thumb over her mouth. "I wanted to take you to dinner after this."

She touched the side of his face. "Are you still offering?"

"Yes. But it'll have to be tomorrow night now." He scowled.

"What time?"

Their faces grew closer until their noses were only an inch apart.

He gazed into her eyes, and she nearly drowned in the deep, crystal blue of them.

"How about eight?"

"Perfect. Greek time." She grinned.

He captured her mouth for one last intoxicating kiss before stepping out of the pool. Grabbing his towel, he dried off.

Christina followed suit.

He left a minute later.

She dropped into the chair on the balcony, pressing a hand to her chest. She leaned back and could still taste the minty freshness of his mouth. That was one hell of a swimming lesson. She hadn't planned on kissing him and attaching herself to him like a starfish on a rock. It was a spontaneous reaction. He'd pulled her in with those gorgeous eyes and lost puppy dog expression while learning to float.

Christina shook her head. She had it bad for Nathan. What would have happened if Becky hadn't burst into the room? Chills ran down her spine. Then heat streaked through her.

She went to the balcony ledge. How could she have gone from having a burning desire to be a chaste nun the rest of her life to wanting to make love to a man she'd only met a few days before?

She knocked twice on the side of her head before stopping and gaping. Maybe this was a sign… *the* sign of what she would do with the rest of her life.

Gazing at the crowded sidewalks, she rubbed her chin. She needed to speak with Father Apostolos tomorrow. He'd help her sort this out in his own subtle way.

Chapter Twenty-Three

Donned in brown cargo shorts, a T-shirt, and his sandals, Nathan hurried toward his uncle's shop. He checked his watch. It wasn't quite six yet. *Thío* Ioannis should still be there getting ready to go fishing.

He reached the door and knocked.

A minute later, his uncle appeared with raised brows. The door swung open.

"Nathan, my boy, what you doing here so early?"

Nathan stepped into the shop.

His uncle had on his sailor's cap and held a fishing pole in his hand. "You know I go fishing this time in morning. And you finish your work yesterday."

"I know, *Thío*." Nathan straightened his back and smiled. He couldn't wait to see his uncle's expression. "I came to go fishing with you."

Thío Ioannis's mouth fell open before his face lit up like a Christmas tree. A huge grin spread across his face, his eyes dancing. He pulled Nathan into a half bear hug. "This is great! When you change your mind?"

"Last night." The arousing swimming lesson with Christina

came back to him, causing his body to react in an embarrassing way, and heat crept into his cheeks.

His uncle slapped his back. "I go get you a pole." He ambled to his office.

Nathan calmed himself by pacing the floor and concentrating on preparing himself to board his uncle's small boat. He could do this now, thanks to Christina. Heat streaked through him. He raised his hands toward the ceiling, gazing up. *Calm down and keep focused.*

Thío Ioannis returned with another pole and handed it to him. He then gestured toward the front door before walking toward it. "Let's go." He grinned. "The fish are biting."

Ten minutes later, Nathan tentatively stepped into his uncle's boat. It rocked under his weight, making his heart skip a beat and his breath come in short spurts. He carefully sat on one of two benches and quickly pulled on a life jacket that lay next to him. He pushed back the horrid memories of the disastrous boat tour. The turquoise water was calm this morning with little waves rolling on the surface. The weather was nothing like that day. He exhaled out his worry.

Thío Ioannis sat at the stern, working to start the motor. Once it rumbled to life, he directed them about a quarter of a mile across the Aegean from the harbor. He cut the motor and set up the bait on their rods.

The light, salty breeze felt cool on Nathan's face as he gazed at the quiet caldera. Nobody was wandering the streets at this time. Only a couple of other small boats bobbed a good distance from them. The morning's misty silence mixed with the pink sunrise relaxed Nathan. With such beauty around him, a part of him regretted not having his painting supplies with him. He'd have to remember to come out on the harbor another time and capture this serene scene.

Thío Ioannis handed him a pole and jutted his chin toward him. "Watch me, and you learn quickly."

"Okay."

His uncle tossed out the line and reeled it in, inch by inch. He turned and looked at Nathan. "Now you try."

Nathan flung out the line, but it dropped only a few feet from him.

Thío Ioannis let out a gravelly laugh. "Keep trying. You get."

Eventually Nathan had swung the pole and cast out the line far enough to his uncle's liking, and he sat in contentment. With the beautiful landscape around him, the rosy rays of the sun warming the side of his face, and the comforting bond with his uncle growing, Nathan now understood why fishing with him had been so important.

Christina's pretty face surfaced in his mind. *Thank you, my love.* The words flowed out of his head without a thought. *My love.* He tensed. Was she? When had that happened? Could it really be true? His throbbing heart told him so. *I hope this relationship works. I need it to.*

MIDAFTERNOON, CHRISTINA ENTERED THE CHURCH, FINDING FATHER Apostolos in his usual spot in the narthex.

"Father, I'm so glad to see you here."

He grinned, with both wrinkled hands on his cane. "You have resolved one of your obstacles, closed off one of the possible paths to your future."

She squatted in front of him. "Yes, I have."

"You have much on your mind and heart today."

"Yes, again." Christina sat on the marble floor. "But I believe I've found my path."

He only gazed at her, his eyes twinkling.

"The man I've met is wonderful, so special, so kind."

He nodded slowly. "Yet you still have the other path open to you that set your heart afire with purpose before meeting this gentleman."

She sighed. "It's not burning as strongly now."

"What do you think that means?"

"I don't know." She covered his hand with hers. "I was hoping you could help me sort out my feelings."

"You must allow God to lead you. I am but a foolish, feeble old man. I am not graced with such a gift."

"But you seem to know so much."

He lifted his chin. "I know nothing."

Frowning, her head dizzy with confusion, Christina took her time to stand. "So, it is still the path of monasticism or the path toward love of a man."

"Pray, and He will reveal your path if you so desire His help."

She bent and kissed his right hand. "I'll try, Father."

"It is all He ever asks of us." He raised his hand and blessed her. "God be with you."

"Thank you."

Christina stepped onto the sidewalk and headed back to her hotel. She'd be meeting Nathan for dinner in a couple of hours. She wanted to take a hot shower and change into something pretty for him this evening. A nice sundress was in order.

Entering her hotel room, she passed the desk and opened the wardrobe to pull out fresh underwear from one of the drawers. She froze, then swung around. The desk was bare. Where had her painting gone? Torn pieces of paper littered the floor below the desk.

Rushing to the scattered scraps, she picked them up one by one and set them on the desk's surface. Another painting ruined. Who'd do such a thing? And why hadn't she stowed it away with the others?

Putting the pieces together like a puzzle, she found a red X across this picture as well. Anger bubbled inside her. Justin hadn't bothered her for the past couple of days, and he didn't care about her "hobby." Who did? She clutched the sides of her head, fisting bunches of hair in each hand.

What about her original painting of Nathan? Icy fear slid through her stomach.

Christina ran back to the bureau and opened the second drawer. The painting was still there. She exhaled, pressing a hand to her chest, then snatched the picture. A new hiding place was needed. Scanning the room, her gaze came back to the drawers. She placed the paper underneath her clothes in the bottom drawer, closed it, then shut the wardrobe's large doors.

The balcony. Christina spun toward the balcony's door and found it closed but not locked. She knew it had been locked since last night. She inspected the flimsy lock on the door handle. Someone must have picked it to get into her room. Goose bumps popped up all over her arms and legs. Why was someone obsessed with her artwork? It made no sense.

Nathan. She needed to see him now. Grabbing her hotel card key, Christina flung the door open and ran down the hall. She rapped on his door in quick succession.

Becky appeared at the door. "Honey, you're as white as whipped cream on a chocolate sundae."

Christina's stomach churned. "Where's Nathan?"

Becky opened the door wide and moved to the side.

Nathan came to the door. "Christina? What is it?"

Just the sight of him gave her comfort. She embraced him, clinging to his body, inhaling the fresh, citrusy scent of him.

He encircled her in his strong arms and kissed her forehead. "What's going on?"

She took his hand and led him back to her room.

"You okay?"

Christina opened the door and pulled him inside. She showed him the ripped paper on the desk. "Somebody tore up my drawing of you."

He picked up one of the pieces, and his face brightened. "I didn't know you had drawn me." He smiled, his eyes shining with affection, before his face fell. "Why did someone tear this up?"

She put a shaky palm to her forehead and paced the floor. "I don't know, but it's the second time it's happened."

"Second time?" Nathan rubbed his chin. "I don't understand. Why would your artwork be vandalized?"

She rushed to the balcony door and jiggled its handle. "And whoever the vandalizer is has been breaking into my room through this door." She pointed at the little lock. "It's not hard to do, as you can see."

He bent and examined the knob. "That's a pretty worthless lock. Might as well not have one." He straightened and shook his head.

"I know." Christina moved back to her drawing and held up her hands. "The whole thing is creepy." She stabbed a finger at the red X across the torn paper. "That makes it even more creepy."

He grimaced. "Somebody doesn't like pictures of me. Terrific."

Her frustration and fear lessened. He looked so cute with that wounded expression. Her heart expanded. She wrapped her arms around his neck. "Let's get out of here, go to dinner, dancing, the works."

Nathan opened his mouth to speak, but she pressed her lips against his and closed her eyes. The heat generated from their kiss nearly made her knees buckle.

"Before we go, don't you think you better report this break-in to the hotel manager?" he said against her mouth.

She paused and opened her eyes. "You're right." She slid the hotel key in her skirt pocket. "I'll meet you in the front of the hotel after I talk to the manager."

He moved toward the door. "See you in a few." He blew her a kiss before slipping out of the room.

A minute later, she left her room, her body still tingling from his kiss. She'd get this mess cleared up quickly and be back with him in no time. He was what she needed.

Chapter Twenty-Four

After a delicious meal of souvlaki, rice, and green beans with tomatoes at Athena Delights restaurant, Christina and Nathan joined a line of dancers making a wide circle on the patio twinkling with its string of white lights. A live band rocked the space, the bouzouki player making the instrument sing with its high-pitched staccato.

Crowds surrounded Christina, their chatter and laughter mixing with the music. Joy buoyed her heart as she bounced from one foot to the other, kicking side to side, as Nathan on her right and a woman on her left did the same in unison.

Groups of people seated at their tables clapped to the music and called out, "Opa!"

The line broke off, and couples came together as the song ended and switched to a slow, romantic melody. Christina hugged Nathan and pressed her cheek against his upper chest, sighing, drunk on happiness.

Nathan kissed her neck and gently ran his hand down her long hair, his other hand against the small of her back. Her body floated from his tender touch. She smiled, pressing her fingers into his back.

If she hadn't been in such a hurry, she would have slipped into that dazzling, red sundress with the plunging back, and his hand would've been against her bare skin. But her white blouse and red skirt would have to do.

She gazed at the beautiful tangerine-and-lavender sky, and a thought came to her. Her body heated and tingled as a dreamy picture of her and Nathan lying on the precipice, cuddled under blankets below the star-studded sky swirled in her head.

Slipping a hand behind Nathan's neck, she leaned her mouth toward his ear. "Do you want to do some collaborating at the lookout tonight?"

Nathan held her closer, his breath against her ear. "What do you have in mind?"

She closed her eyes and smiled, her cheek against his. "Sleeping under the stars."

He let out a throaty chuckle. "Sounds perfect."

They left the floor and headed toward the restaurant's exit, with hands intertwined.

THEY SETTLED ON A BLANKET AT THE PRECIPICE. THE SETTING SUN'S violet rays bathed their faces. Nathan wrapped his arms around Christina, his legs pressing against hers, her back leaning against his chest. The late evening's breeze fanned their bodies, and below them, lit-up boats sprinkled the undulating dark blue water.

Christina sighed. "Being with you takes away all my worries."

A picture of Christina sitting next to him in this very spot days ago, telling him about her former marriage and loss of her baby filled his head. He closed his eyes. It was only fair he should share his past with her too. And this seemed the right time.

He scooted away from her, stood, and faced the caldera. The scene with Jennifer played like a video in his head again. Nobody knew about what had happened, except George. Not even Nathan's parents. He'd been too ashamed to tell them. Thankfully, as big a loudmouth as George was, he was Fort Knox when it came to private matters.

He closed his eyes and exhaled. If he wanted something real and long-lasting with Christina, he needed to be honest with her.

Her arms encircled his waist, and she pressed her chest against his back. "What's wrong?"

He froze, his body tense. Would she hate him if he told her, now knowing a painful part of her past? He swallowed the fear lodged in his throat. He gritted his teeth. *Quit being a coward. Just be honest, forthright. It's the best way to do this.* He turned to face her, taking her hands in his. "I need to tell you something, but I'm afraid how you're going to take it."

Her ebony eyes appeared to glow with concern, the corners of her mouth turning slightly down. "You don't want to spend time with me anymore, do you?"

Nathan squeezed her hands. "God, no. The total opposite." He ran a gentle hand over the side of her face. "I love being with you."

A smile broke on her face, clearing away the furrowed lines on her forehead.

He pointed to the blanket. "Let's sit back down."

"Okay."

She settled on the blanket and waited for him to join her.

He sat next to her, and after gazing into her eyes, he focused on the dark water glistening in the moonlight. Clasping his hands in his lap, his stomach roiled.

"I had a girlfriend for about a year, but we broke up five months ago."

Christina said nothing, just looked at him as if waiting for him to continue.

Nathan wiped his damp palms on his thighs. *Just get to the point.* He blew out a breath. "Jennifer ended up pregnant six months into our dating."

Anguish swirled in Christina's dark eyes, and his heart ached over causing her pain.

He smoothed down her hair, his hand pausing at the nape of her neck. He brought his forehead to hers, closing his eyes. "I'm sorry. I don't mean to stir up your own hurts."

She ran her hand over his stubbly cheek. "It's okay. I can tell you need to get out whatever it is that's bothering you."

He lifted his head from hers, locked his gaze with hers, and swallowed hard. "She didn't want to be pregnant." He hurried ahead as Christina's face drained of color. "She said her parents would have a conniption over her being pregnant and not married. She told me her only choice was to have an abortion."

Christina's eyes glistened with tears. His heart wrenched in his chest, his own pain mingling with the hurt he believed she was feeling too.

"I told her we could get married. I'd help take care of our baby. I'd already planned to ask her to marry me anyway. I'd just been saving up for a nice engagement ring." He looked away, his jaw tightening, remembering Jennifer's obstinate reaction and stony expression. "But she said she wasn't ready to get married. Didn't know if she ever would marry." He wiped his palms across his legs again. "She'd never mentioned that until then. I felt blindsided, lost."

While he stared at his hands, Christina sniffled. He couldn't look at her now. Shame burned his cheeks and sweat gathered on his forehead.

"What did she end up doing?" she asked in a shaky voice.

He exhaled a heavy breath. "We argued for three days. I repeatedly told her I'd help her raise the child, married or not. She kept harping on about not wanting to disappoint her parents and having to abort the baby. She pleaded with me that I support her decision. Eventually she wore me down by saying she'd leave me if I didn't support her."

"My God, Nathan..." Christina's voice was only a whisper.

"I foolishly thought if I agreed, someday in the future, she'd change her mind about marrying me. That she'd see how I stuck by her through it all and happily want to make that next important step with me. So, I said I'd support her even though the thought of what she was going to do with our baby made me sick to my stomach, and everything inside me felt it was the wrong decision, that I shouldn't have backed down."

Queasiness rolled through his stomach, remembering the heartache and his regretful response. He swallowed back bitterness, got up, and paced the grassy area next to Christina and the blanket.

"I can't imagine how hard that was... the pressure..."

He paused and raked a hand through his hair. "She had the procedure done. Our relationship wasn't the same after that, and she left me two weeks later."

Nathan clasped his hands together so hard they hurt. "It didn't matter that I gave in. She still left me. It was then I realized she never really cared about me or us. I didn't count in her world. She'd had other plans she hadn't bothered to share with me until the pregnancy." He shoved his hands in his shorts pockets. "The pathetic thing was I never saw through her total disregard for our relationship until it was put in front of me like a flashing traffic light. What mattered to her was her reputation in the eyes of her parents and her elite social circles."

Christina came to him, moving in front of his view of the caldera. She put her arms around his neck, her hands digging in his hair. She gazed up at him with a look of empathy, not pity. Exactly what he'd needed. Understanding and loving. He folded her in his arms, and their lips met.

She moved back an inch. "I'm so sorry." Tears welled in her eyes again.

He ran his hand over her chin. "I know this must have really stung, seeing how you wanted your baby and..."

She put a finger to his lips. "It wasn't easy, but it's not your fault." Her eyes locked on his. "I have a feeling you haven't shared this with many people."

"Only George."

She nodded. "I understand."

They embraced again before Nathan bent to fold the blanket. The mood was ruined.

Christina put a hand on his wrist. "We can still lie here under the stars, can't we?"

He paused. "Are you sure?"

"Yes." She gestured toward the grassy spot they'd been sitting on. "Go ahead and spread out that blanket." A smile tugged at the corner of her mouth.

He shook out the throw, and they lay down. Christina curled up against him, her head leaning on his chest. He held her closely at his side.

She pointed at the night sky, sparkling with white gems. "Beautiful. There's life in all of them."

Nathan kissed her forehead and looked at the twinkling stars. "There is."

Christina laced her hand with his, and they lay in silence, watching the sky, until Christina's breathing became soft and regular.

He smiled. Christina understood him, cared about him. She was nothing like Jennifer. He welcomed the light night breeze sweeping across his face. There was a good chance their relationship could work. *Damn it. I want that more than anything.* He kissed her forehead, then closed his eyes, allowing the sounds of the sea below, the aroma of the surrounding flowers and briny air to fill his senses, as he savored the moment.

Chapter Twenty-Five

While Nathan was out fishing with his uncle, Christina sat across from Becky at a restaurant's patio two buildings down from their hotel.

"George is out of concussion prison, so we'll be frolicking on the beach in a couple of hours." Becky took a sip of coffee, then grinned. "Return of the mer-people."

Christina chuckled, setting down her half-eaten piece of toast. "Freedom."

"You better believe it."

"I believe it."

"Seems you had a bit of freedom last night." Becky winked.

Her cheeks warmed. "Freedom to fall asleep under the stars."

"Cozy cuddles dreams are made of."

"You better believe it." Christina winked.

Becky snorted.

Small groups of people wandered the sidewalks—too early for the mob of tourists to be cluttering the streets.

Justin appeared at the Dolphin Hotel's front door and headed toward a cab idling at the curb. He held three bulky suitcases, and sunglasses shielded his expressionless face.

"Hope he's not going to come over here." Christina folded her napkin.

Becky looked up from her bowl of yogurt with honey. "Who?"

"Who do you think?" Christina pointed at Justin, who was tossing his bags into the back seat of the car.

"Don't worry. The snake seems to be slithering back to his hole in Denver." Becky pointed her spoon at Christina. "Your wish has been granted, dear one."

Before Justin opened the front passenger door, his head turned in Christina's direction, and he spotted her.

She groaned.

"Quit looking his way. Act like you didn't see him," Becky said, scrunching over her bowl as if that position would hide her.

Justin gave her a farewell salute, climbed in the taxi, and it rolled slowly away.

Christina pressed a hand to her chest and sighed.

Becky rubbed her hands together as if brushing them clean of food remnants. "The relic is shelved at last."

Her stomach settled, and she smiled.

"What are your plans for the day?"

"I'm going to chur—"

"Yeah." Becky waved a hand. "Besides church."

Christina shrugged. "I'm not sure."

"What? No plans with Nathan?"

Her heart ballooned at the sound of his name. "He's spending most of the day with his uncle. I'm sure I'll see him later today."

"Can't believe we're leaving Greece in a few days. Our vacation flew by, most of it ruined by George's knocking himself silly."

Christina finished her *portakolada* and signaled the waiter passing their table. "Check please."

The waiter nodded and scuttled back into the restaurant.

"See you back at the hotel tonight?" Becky asked, pushing her chair in.

"Of course."

Christina strolled with Becky until they reached their hotel, and Becky slipped into its lobby.

She continued toward the church.

Father Apostolos was sitting in his usual chair in the narthex. No one else was in the church. She bent and kissed his right hand. "Morning, Father."

"Good morning, my child." He patted her bowed head.

She squatted in front of him, beaming. "I've found my path."

"God has led you to it?"

"I believe so. Too many signs to ignore."

He nodded. His face held a sober expression, much more serious than she'd ever seen before.

Her stomach knotted. Was she misinterpreting God's guideposts again?

She stood, wringing her hands. "Is something wrong, Father?"

He clasped the handle to his cane and looked up at her, his eyes nearly colorless. "Beware of your surroundings. Walk with care."

Chills rained over her body. "Father, what do you mean?"

With trembling hands leaning on his cane, he got up from the chair. "Take heed of what I've told you, my child."

"I'm trying. I…" Christina stood rigid, unable to move.

The elder lifted his right hand, blessed her, then hobbled out of the church's entryway.

Shaking free from her stunned position, she hurried to the entrance. Outside, the sparsely populated streets held no evidence of Father Apostolos's little black-robed body having walked its alabaster sidewalks.

She pressed fists to the sides of her head. How did he keep doing that? If she hadn't seen him, touched him, she'd have thought he wasn't real. His appearances and disappearances made no sense to her. Yet, for the majority of the time she'd needed to see him, he had been there. What was this all about?

She tapped her temples. *Don't try to figure it out. It'll drive you crazy.* She glanced back at the church's foyer. "Just remember what he said even if you don't understand."

Looking both ways four times before crossing the street, Christina headed back to her hotel.

Chapter Twenty-Six

C hristina pushed the door to her hotel room open and stepped over a folded piece of paper on the floor. She picked it up and flipped it open.

> Dear Christina,
>
> Meet me at the lookout at 4:00 p.m. Bring your art stuff.
>
> Nathan

She smiled. Another artistic collaboration at the precipice. *Perfect.* She set the paper on the desk and headed to the bathroom for a refreshing shower.

CHRISTINA WADED THROUGH THE WILDFLOWERS TO THEIR USUAL SPOT by the cliff facing the caldera and yellow-and-blue horizon. Nathan wasn't there yet.

A strong breeze came off the water, washing over her face, and every pore in her body absorbed its briny scent.

She set down her art bag and breathed in the warm air. Putting her hands against her lower back, she arched, stretching, enjoying the scene of bobbing fishing boats on the cerulean Aegean below.

Shoes crunched the gravelly ground behind her, causing her heartbeat to race with anticipation.

Christina grinned and spun around, coming face-to-face with Thalia.

"Oh," she muttered.

Thalia smirked and crossed her arms. "Hello, Christina."

"Hi. What are you doing here?"

The woman didn't answer but snatched Christina's art bag. "You remember all your art things?"

Christina tensed. How did she know she was here? That she'd planned to draw while Nathan painted? A frightening thought came to her, iciness sliding down her spine. Her torn paintings. The break-ins. Had the culprit been Thalia, not Justin?

Thalia stuck her head in the bag. "Hmm." She lifted her head and squeezed the top of the bag closed with both hands. "Yes. Look like all of art there."

What game was this woman playing? A slow simmer of anger streaked through her. "Why are you here, Thalia?"

Again, the woman didn't answer. She walked to the edge of the rocky cliff and, with a swing of her arm, tossed Christina's art tote over the side.

Too stunned to move at first, Christina gaped before she rushed to the ledge and spotted her battered bag lying in a pile of crumbled stones and trash behind a tiny white house. Her art supplies were scattered over the garbage thirty feet below her.

She turned to face Thalia, still trying to digest what Nathan's good friend had just done. Was she crazy? "Why did you do that?"

Thalia smiled with smugness. "You no good at art."

"How do—?"

"And Nathan not coming."

Thalia stepped in front of her, so close she could smell fish on the woman's breath, and the tiny specks of gold tints in her irises glistened back at her.

"What are—?"

Nathan's friend moved even closer to her, forcing Christina to back up, her heel off the edge of the lookout. She struggled with her balance, light-headedness hitting her.

"Nathan my friend, not yours." Thalia's eyes darkened, and the lines around her mouth creased, her lips in a flat, firm line. "He mine."

Christina clasped her shaking hands to steady them. She needed to defuse the situation. "Of course. I know you've been friends since you were children."

"I know him and what he needs," Thalia said, hissing. She narrowed her eyes and lifted her chin, looking her up and down. "You no good for him."

She put her hands on her hips and huffed in Christina's face. Afraid of losing her balance, Christina pulled her hands apart and reached for Thalia's arms.

Thalia slapped Christina's hands before they reached her shoulders. The woman's lip curled in a snarl before she let out a laugh. "You know Nathan so good you can't read his writing." Her giggles turned into snorts, and her finger shot out, pointing at Christina's chest.

Startled by her maniacal cackling and sudden movement, Christina jerked backward.

Scrambling for her balance, Christina slipped off the cliff, a scream ripping out of her throat. She flailed her arms, reaching for anything on the side of the steep, rocky terrain to grab and stop her fast descent.

Tears stung her eyes as she groped for branches of a bush above a jutting boulder. She caught hold of a couple of the stringy limbs. Her body jerked, flinging her against the rocky wall, knocking the breath out of her. She sucked in air, her heart nearly galloping out of her heaving chest. The wild vines stretched out as she held on to them with all her strength and dug her foot in the small dirt crevice above the big stone.

She stood on one foot in a hunched position not daring to look down. As her heartbeat pounded in her ears, she took the chance to peer at the blurry ledge five feet above her. The tears that had welled in her eyes and were now streaming down her cheeks made it almost impossible to make out Thalia's figure standing near the cliff's edge.

Through blurred vision, Christina yelled, "Thalia, help me!"

The figure on the ledge bent, and Christina's eyes cleared enough to make out Thalia.

Nathan's friend pressed her hands to the sides of her head, her mouth ajar. "*Skatá*!" she shrieked, her tone singed with a mixture of shock and fear.

Thalia retreated from the ledge.

Christina's heart sank as the cold reality hit her like ice water to the face. Thalia wasn't going to help her.

She scanned the area around her for some way to climb back up the side of the caldera. She couldn't stay there forever. Her arms were beginning to ache, and the twisty thin branches gave her little confidence they would hold her much longer. Her foot tingled, tiny needles pricking it all over.

She sniffled. What could she do?

Fresh tears spilled down her cheeks, as she shifted her focus to the little white chapel to her left. The door opened, and Father Apostolos stepped out the entryway and gazed at her. His body glowed white with a blue light outlining his small figure.

Christina gasped. "Father." Her heart ached as she took in gulps of air. "Help me." She wasn't able to shout loud enough for him to hear over the distance and wind.

The elder's words came back to her. *Beware of your surroundings. Walk with care.*

She squeezed her eyes shut, working to clear her vision. She focused on the priest again. He hadn't moved, but he lifted his hand in a blessing. What was he doing? Why wasn't he coming to her aid?

His bright form disappeared before her eyes.

Her mouth hung open. "Dear God."

"Thalia, what are you—?"

Nathan! He's up there!

"Hey, come back," he said.

"Nathan! Help me!" Christina screamed as loudly as she could.

Nathan appeared at the edge of the lookout and peered down at her. "Christina! Jesus!"

Her eyes filmed over with mist again. "Help me!" Her arms burned—the muscles so tight, little tremors radiated through them. Her hands cramped, palms pulsating and sore. Grimacing through the pain, she didn't know how much longer she could keep holding on.

He lay down, his chest hanging over the cliff, and stretched his arms toward her. "Can you reach my hands?"

Nathan's hands were a couple of feet above her. How would she be able to grab hold of them? If she let go of the vines, she'd fall.

Something solid pushed against her bottom, moving her in Nathan's direction. The weight under her emanated warmth and strength. What was happening? The branches were straight across from her chest now, her foot off the stone, dangling with the solid form below her still pressing her steadily upward.

Swallowing, she spared a glance below her. Father Apostolos's glowing, bent form hovered under her, using his back to push her skyward. She squinted against the shining white of his figure.

Peace permeated her whole body, then settled in her heart. Christina closed her eyes and exhaled slowly. She let go of the vines and joined her hands with Nathan's, and he pulled her up while the elder continued to lift her from the rear.

She climbed over the ledge and rolled on the ground, ending up in Nathan's arms. He embraced her tightly, his thumping chest against hers.

Father Apostolos peeked over the cliff, his face beaming with light. "God be with you, my child."

Nathan gaped as she sat up with him, their arms still around each other.

The elder's beautiful, childlike face vanished, leaving the caldera and horizon before them.

The peace inside Christina floated out of her. She clung to Nathan. "The elder and you saved me. Thank you." She hugged him with the little strength she had left, the solidness of his body against hers spreading relief through her.

Nathan cupped both sides of her face and gave her a gentle kiss.

"Saint Paul the Cave Dweller," he said.

"What?"

"You didn't recognize him?"

"No." Christina gazed at the chapel as memories from church school came back to her. Saint Paul the Cave Dweller lived in the fifteenth century on the island of Paros. He was known for helping those looking for guidance in their career and life endeavors.

She covered her mouth. She'd been talking to a wonder-working saint the whole while. That explained why the tourists who would enter the church never seemed to notice him. They hadn't seen him, only she had. She gazed up at Nathan. So had he.

The draw and connection between them intensified as her eyes welled with tears again, and she nodded. "I understand."

Nathan got up with his hand in hers, helping her stand. With his arm protectively around her shoulder and hers around his waist, they turned toward the town's street a few yards away.

"I heard you talking to Thalia," she said, a shiver vibrating through her.

"Yeah. She was facing the caldera when I approached and spoke to her. But then she took off like her ass was on fire."

She stiffened as angry heat flooded her. "She didn't help me when I fell."

His jaw twitched, his stare hard as steel. "I figured that out after I found you." He squeezed her against his side, the gesture seemingly a delayed protective reaction to what had happened.

"She told me you were hers and I was no good for you."

He gently rubbed his hands up and down her arms. "She lied." He kissed her forehead twice before enveloping her in a warm hug.

She clung to him, taking in the smell of him, the feel of him, the love of him.

Comforted, she peered at the caldera. The precipice gave her chills when it had taken her breath away and delighted her the day before. She burrowed against his chest, his strong arms holding her again.

The terrible events flashed through her mind, starting with Thalia throwing her art tote off the ledge. She needed to get to it somehow.

Christina gazed up at him. "She threw my art bag off the cliff." She pointed toward the grassy ledge.

His jaw dropped. "What?" He shook his head. "She's not the girl I remember."

"She was a child then. A long time ago."

"Yeah. Shows how much a person can change over the years."

She nodded. "My bag will need a good washing, but I can't leave without it."

He ran his hands over the sides of her face, then kissed her nose. "Wouldn't think of leaving it behind."

She moved with him onto the alabaster walkway, grateful for him and Saint Paul. Without them, she might not have been walking away from that lookout but left with broken bones or, worse, dead. She swallowed hard, and exhaustion settled in every bone and muscle of her body.

Christina leaned her head against Nathan's shoulder and focused on retrieving her tote.

Chapter Twenty-Seven

C hristina sat on her bed and packed her suitcase while Becky did the same.

"Still can't believe what happened to you," Becky said with a shake of her head. "If I'd been there, that coward, Thalia, would've swallowed a fist sandwich."

Christina grinned. "My heroine."

Becky pointed at her. "You better believe it. Nobody tries to take out my best friend without losing teeth and gaining a permanent limp."

She laughed. "Well, you can't beat a holy saint coming to your rescue."

"Okay, I'll give you that." Becky closed her luggage. "Un-freaking-believable. Just wish I had been there to see that."

"It's been three days, and it still feels surreal."

Becky tilted her head to the side. "Guess that was a big surprise to Nathan. His friend turned into a wacky wild woman in a matter of days."

"He was, but like I told him, he hadn't seen her since they were kids."

"Somewhere in between, Ms. Jekyll had turned into Ms. Hyde."

"Seems so."

Becky waved a hand in dismissal. "Well, it's history now, and we're off to Athens."

Christina took her original painting of Nathan from the wardrobe and carefully slid it into her sketchbook in her art bag. She'd figure a clever way to sneak her colored drawing to Nathan, wanting it to be a surprise.

She smiled and zipped up her suitcase, then frowned, knowing they were going home in a couple of days, uncertain when she'd see Nathan again. She ran her hand across the cloth of her floral-designed luggage. She couldn't imagine losing him. He'd come into her life for a reason.

She went out on the balcony, the bright sun nearly blinding her. The rolling, blue waves of the sea in the distance seemed to match the roiling of her stomach.

Wait. Her mouth opened in realization. How had she forgotten their meeting had been kismet? A sign? Even Father Apostolos... er, Saint Paul, had pretty much agreed. Hadn't he?

The elder had only warned her about Thalia in his own cryptic way. He'd asked her if God had led her to the path toward a true loving relationship with Nathan. He hadn't confirmed or denied what she believed was her right path.

But Nathan had shown up at the precipice, and he'd told her something had prodded him—urged him—to go there to paint. Perhaps the saint had nudged Nathan in some mystical sense. Yes, he must have. To be there to help her.

Her heart bloomed as Nathan pulling her off the ledge came back to her. The warm, tingling streaming through her couldn't be mistaken. They had a real connection. Where would it lead after they left Greece?

Two days later in Athens, Nathan grabbed his bag off the seat and climbed out of the taxi.

Modest ivory homes flanked the road, with several trees wedged between the houses like natural fences.

His grandfather's white, two-story house with its large, open windows, one with a balcony off of it, looked the same as when he'd stayed in it during his childhood. The small patch of front lawn was trimmed and lush. Flowerpots sat on the balcony's ledge and on either side of the solid pearl-colored front door.

More memories of the summers spent with his grandfather flooded his mind. Images of Papou cutting up watermelon on a platter for him and his brother sitting at his kitchen table made him smile. All the trips to the souvlaki and ice cream vendors near his grandfather's home. He licked his lips, still tasting the delicious meat and sweet, creamy frozen dessert. He and his brother used to race each other to the park and mini golf course. His older brother beat him nearly every time, but it'd all been good, clean fun.

He approached the door that was cracked open and knocked on it.

The door opened, and his grandfather appeared, with a generous grin revealing coffee-stained teeth. In his seventies, Papou had a heavy-set figure with thinning gray hair, a double chin, and piercing blue eyes.

"Nathan *mou. Ti kanís*?" His grandfather gathered him into a bear hug and kissed both his cheeks, the smell of mint on his breath.

"Hey, Papou. I'm doing well." He pointed at his grandfather. "You're looking well too."

Papou laid his hands on his chubby chest. "Not too bad." He crooked an arm toward the inside of the house. "Come inside."

Nathan followed his grandfather and George into the white-tiled foyer.

His grandfather moved to the living room with its beige couch and two chairs. "Sit down."

Nathan sat on the sofa just as his grandfather lowered himself next to him, then clapped a hand on his back. "I'm so happy to see you. It's been too long. How's the family?"

"Good."

"Aha." He grinned and nodded.

"You want something to drink? Soda? Water, Nathan *mou*?"

"Water's fine, Papou. *Efcharistó*."

Papou rose slowly from the couch. His joints crackled.

Nathan cringed and touched his grandfather's arm. "I'll get the drinks. The glasses are in the same cabinet, right?" He was already moving toward the doorway to the kitchen.

His grandfather let out a sigh and settled back on the couch. "Yes. You always a good boy, Nathan."

He came back with the glasses and handed one to his grandfather.

Nathan set his drink on the table in front of the sofa, then carefully unzipped his large travel bag. He pulled out the shiny wood worry beads and held them up. He flashed a wide grin. "A fresh set for your fingers to wear down."

"Ah." Papou tapped his finger to his temple. "Such a thoughtful grandson." He took the beads and rolled them between his pudgy palms. He brought them to his nose and inhaled their aroma, then chuckled. "One of the best smells."

Nathan peeked inside his bag for his ultimate gift. The painting took up a large portion of his luggage, wrapped in brown packaging paper. A white, sleek ribbon ran vertically and horizontally across the rectangular object. He pulled it out of the bag and set it on his lap.

His grandfather's bushy gray brows rose. "What is this?"

"I've finally finished the painting."

His grandfather's mouth fell open. "Yiayia?"

Nathan nodded and handed the package to him.

Running his fingers over the paper, Papou sniffled and looked at Nathan. He leaned toward him and patted his leg. "*Efcharistó*, Nathan *mou*." He pulled off the ribbon and paper then glided a hand over the painting's carved wooden frame. "*Panemorfi*."

"Yes."

Papou's gaze went back to the painting of Yiayia. "She look so alive, so beautiful. Just as I remember her." He studied Nathan's face. "You make her come alive for me." His eyes glistened with tears before he gave Nathan a gentle pat on the cheek. "You are a gifted artist, *asteri mou*."

Pride filled his heart. He'd given his grandfather something of Yiayia he could cherish forever. He smiled. "*Efcharistó*, Papou."

His grandfather rose from the couch and shuffled over to the wall across from him. He propped up the painting against the white space. "We put it up here or in my bedroom?"

"It's up to you."

Papou glanced at the large window letting in the bright sunshine that hit the painting just at the right angle that its vivid colors glittered. "We put it up here."

"Sounds good." Nathan joined him.

Papou set down the painting and wrapped an arm around Nathan's shoulders. "Yiayia would love this picture, like I do." He planted a big kiss on Nathan's cheek.

Even with the absence of Yiayia still lingering in the room, the sweet memories of him and his grandfather had only grown. Comfort always encapsulated him in his grandfather's house and in his paternal arms. He'd have to come back to see his grandfather again, not let the years go by. They were too precious to waste.

Chapter Twenty-Eight

C hristina shouldered her art bag in Nathan's hotel room, where Becky and George cuddled by the open window, their backs to her.

George glanced over at her. "Nate's still with his grandpa. But he'll come back here for the night."

She nodded. When he focused on the view out the window once more, with Becky pointing at the Acropolis in the distance, Christina scanned the room for Nathan's luggage. She only saw George's bulky knapsack. *Crap.* This would have been the perfect opportunity for her to slip her drawing of him into his bag and sneak back to her and Becky's hotel room.

She tiptoed around the small room, squatting to look under one of the beds.

"Girl, what are you doing?"

She paused from peeking under the bed and looked up at her friend with a sheepish smile. "Looking for dust bunnies?"

The corner of Becky's mouth lifted. "Really? You can do better than that." She bent next to her. "Come on. Spill it. Nathan hasn't had the chance to stow anything under there."

A hearty laugh came from George, his back to the window

now. "Something rockin' under the bed? Wonder what it could be." He sauntered over to them.

Christina shot up. "There's nothing to see."

"Then why were you crawling on the floor to see…" Becky held up two fingers on each hand, gesturing air quotes. "Dust bunnies?" She stood and nudged Christina's arm. She gave her an amused grin.

"I was just wondering where Nathan's suitcase was. I don't see it anywhere—"

"He took it with him to his grandpa's house. He had his painting of his grandma in it." George held up his hand. "Don't worry. He'll be here soon."

Becky draped an arm around her shoulders. "Doubting again?" She wiggled her fingers. "Let it go. Your love life is banging on all cylinders that won't jam up and creak to a stop just because you leave here."

George gestured toward Becky to join him. She left Christina and was nearly swallowed up by his beefy arms encircling her tiny body.

"She's right. We're gonna keep in touch. No way I'm letting this one go." George kissed Becky's forehead.

If only Nathan were here and she could be in his arms like Becky in George's. She moved to the window and gazed out at the sandwiched buildings and crowded streets. Tomorrow morning, they'd be flying back home. What about her artwork? When would she be able to tuck it in his bag before he went to his gate at the airport? She bit her lip. She needed to figure out a way to do that before tomorrow.

"We're leaving for dinner. Come with us," Becky said.

George laid a big hand on Christina's shoulder. "He'll probably be back here in a couple of hours."

Two hours. That would give her plenty of time to stash the picture after dinner. "Okay. Let's go."

"Don't you want to drop off your bag?" Becky asked.

"Oh no." Christina chuckled and patted her tote. "I'll just bring it with me."

"You're more attached to that thing ever since Thalia the Terrible tossed it over the cliff. Don't blame you. I'd be walking with that bag pasted to my side until I got home. I know how much your art means to you." Becky nodded and held a thumbs-up.

Christina smiled and followed her friend out the door with George behind her.

AFTER DINNER, GEORGE AND BECKY HAD GONE FOR ONE LAST STROLL on the busy sidewalks while Christina headed to Nathan's hotel room.

When she reached the glass doors to the hotel, a cab drove up to the curb. Nathan stepped out, turned, and pulled out his luggage from the back seat.

"Nathan." Christina ran and embraced him.

He gave her a gentle kiss. "My favorite person." He jutted his chin toward the hotel's entrance. "Come on."

In his room, Christina stood by the window while Nathan went to the bathroom. She tiptoed to his suitcase lying on one of the beds and slipped her drawing inside it.

Like Becky, Nathan hadn't thought it strange that Christina had carried around her art tote. She set it on the nightstand between the beds and walked to the window again, as the large orange moon hung over the Acropolis, its rays bathing the building.

She heard Nathan's bare feet moving across the wood floor toward his bed. A few minutes later, his arms wrapped around her waist, and he kissed her neck.

She turned and circled his neck with her arms, then frowned. "I can't believe we're leaving tomorrow morning."

He tucked strands of her hair behind her ear. "I know. But we agreed to set up a weekend to see each other once we're home."

She nodded, then lowered her head. His hand caressed her cheek before lifting her chin. Their lips met, and the kiss deepened. Her body morphed into a marshmallow, and she floated, her head swimming.

The door to the room opened, and George and Becky entered with hands intertwined. Christina broke the kiss, and Nathan turned toward his friend.

Becky gestured to Christina. "Let's go. We've got to be up by four."

Before Christina's stomach could turn into a butterfly pavilion, she hugged Nathan again, then grabbed her art tote and crossed to the door where Becky was.

All the signs said she and Nathan had a future ahead of them. She'd let go, like Becky always said, and let fate take over, a sweet fate she cheered on. Her past desires for monasticism had dissipated like morning mist evaporating in the sun. It had never been a bad path to tread down, but it wasn't her path. Just because she'd been divorced after an impulsive marriage didn't mean she couldn't find a true, loving relationship full of hope and mutual respect. She had.

NATHAN WIPED AWAY THE TEARS ROLLING DOWN CHRISTINA'S cheeks. They stood at the departure gates, theirs conveniently adjacent to each other.

He held her, inhaling her tangerine, flowery scent, and buried his face in her hair. "Have a safe trip, and I'll call you when I'm back home," he said.

She gazed up at him with wet eyes. "Promise?"

"Promise."

His lips met hers, and he savored the taste of her mouth,

hoping that it would linger as long as possible while traveling home.

Their lips parted, and she gave him a quivering smile. "Safe travels to you and George too."

She turned to go, but he caught her arm. She looked at him with tears rolling down her face.

"One more thing." He pulled her into his arms one last time and whispered in her ear, "I love you."

Her arms encircled his neck, and she sighed with her cheek against his. "I love you too."

He let her go, and after George and Becky finished their hug, they waved goodbye.

Nathan followed George toward their gate. He'd never forget this vacation. He'd gone there to see his grandfather and uncle, and he'd enjoyed their time together. But meeting Christina had been a once-in-a-lifetime moment. *The moment.* What he'd been looking for all his life. And he hadn't even been looking, but there she'd been, stunning and sweet. A jewel in the midst of all the dull rocks he'd picked through his adult years. He couldn't wait until she saw his painting of her tucked away in her art bag. He'd managed to slip it in last night while she'd been looking out the window.

His heart ready to burst with joy, Nathan found his seat on the plane next to George. He looked out the window at the pink sun rising. Christina had something of his that was one of the most important things to him in his life. His artwork. She also had his heart.

Chapter Twenty-Nine

Christina threw her suitcase on her bed and unzipped it. *Time to unpack.* A knock on the door had her pivoting toward it.

Becky leaned against the frame, grimacing with arms crossed. "Back to work tomorrow. Bummer."

Christina laughed. "Back to reality."

"I liked living in fantasy land."

Christina shrugged, opened her art bag, and removed items out of it. A small canvas at the bottom of the tote caught her attention. Puzzled, she pulled it out, then gasped. An unbelievable likeness of her sitting on the ledge of the lookout with vivid reds, blues, whites, and golds filled the space. Her black hair swayed in the breeze that could be seen in the way he'd applied the brush strokes.

"What? What is it?" Becky hurried over to her and studied the picture. "Holy moly. You've got one talented boyfriend. I'd keep him if I were you." She winked.

Her heart fluttering, Christina held up the artwork with a sense of pride. "No question about that." She scanned her bedroom's walls. "It's going right over here, above the porcelain church."

"Good place for it."

She set the picture on her desk and shook her head, chuckling.

"What's so funny?"

"I put the first painting I did of him at the precipice in his suitcase. I wonder if he was as surprised as me to find my picture."

"Bet you he was, and he's hanging it on his bedroom wall too." Becky grinned.

"I can't wait until next weekend. We're spending it with our guys in Santa Fe."

"You better believe it."

"I believe it." Christina winked.

THAT SAME AFTERNOON, NATHAN EMPTIED HIS SUITCASE, STUMBLING upon Christina's painting of him in the compartment where he'd stashed his art supplies. How had that gotten in there? He grinned. She'd snuck it in his bag just like he had done with his artwork for her. He burst out laughing.

"Man, what're you going on about?" George asked. He filled the doorframe to Nathan's bedroom.

Nathan held up Christina's watercolor drawing of him. The likeness was amazing, the colors glorious. She could draw and paint as well as him. What a pair they made.

George walked toward the picture for a closer look. He whistled. "Got a Monet-ette there, huh?"

"I think I found my soul mate."

"Uh, yeah. You and she were made for each other." George slapped a hand on Nathan's shoulder. "Congrats. I knew you'd find someone after Jennifer if you'd open up again."

The name slid off his back without any meaning. Nathan held the painting against the wall above his desk. "It's going here."

"Yep. That works."

"I'll get to thank her next weekend."

"Yeah. A heap of thanking in all kinds of creative ways, I bet." Nathan grinned. "You'd be right."

Six Months Later

CHRISTINA'S AND NATHAN'S PAINTINGS HUNG NEXT TO EACH OTHER on the wall of a small, local art gallery, holding a showing for the week.

Arms around each other, facing their masterpieces from their vacation, Christina kissed his cheek. "Congratulations, darling."

He kissed her on the mouth. "Congratulations to you, sweetheart."

"Who would have thought our work would make it in the Springs' Local Artists' Gallery?" Christina shook her head, her heart soaring.

"Well, it just tells you we're really that good." Nathan chuckled.

Christina laughed.

He took her left hand in his, the half-carat diamond engagement ring sparkling in the gallery lights. "Our canvas is vast and waiting to be filled with all the colors of our life together."

Christina cocked her head to the side, beaming. "And to think. It all started over paintings with good intentions."

The End

About the Author

Dorothy Robey writes predominantly under her pen name, Dorothea Anna. She is the author of five published books, including her newest one, *Painted With Good Intentions*. Dorothy lives with her family in beautiful Colorado.

https://www.dotluvs2write.com

 facebook.com/dorothy.robey.7
twitter.com/Dotwriter3

Also by Dorothea Anna

Passage of Promise
What She Didn't Know
The Rocky Retreat
Behind the Stone House

"*Painted With Good Intentions* takes the reader on a marvelous journey of self-discovery alongside Nathan and Christina as they learn to expect the unexpected."

— MICHELLE GODARD-RICHER, AUTHOR

"A lovely story that explores what it means to follow your heart and find your intended path."

— TRISHA MESSMER, AUTHOR

CPSIA information can be obtained
at www.ICGtesting.com
Printed in the USA
LVHW042250260422
717240LV00005B/336